color, choosing his words carefully to match, nuance
for nuance, his sometimes-gritty, sometimes-
atmospheric subject matter. Clearly, Smith relishes
both our sumptuous language and life's contradictory,
ambiguous – and wondrous – moments."
David Kaslow
(author of *Living Dangerously with the Horn: Thoughts on
Life and Art*, Horn Professor, Emeritus, Denver University)

❧ ❧ ❧

Views Cost Extra

Short Stories

L.E. Smith

Fomite

Burlington, Vermont

ISBN-13: 978-0-9832063-1-6

Fomite
58 Peru Street
Burlington, VT 05401
www.fomitepress.com
Cover art by Nathania Rubin
Author photograph by Alan Doe

Table of Contents

The Perfect Cowboy Movie

Silence and heat overwhelm the pink sand and chaparral mesquite, saguaro cactus with crimson fruit, and the lonely impress of tire tracks upon which a diamond-back writhes and lizards scramble and cacti bristle. A squatter's trailer faded pale blue nestles in a rock outcrop, its windows shattered and screen door chattering as the wind rises and falls. A small motion of sand begins to dervish and funnel, obscures the view and collapses hinges -- screen door goes off like gunshot -- then scours tin and lifts a corner of the roof, but settles just as soon in a patter of dust upon Daryl Epstein. Daryl is sprawled on the kitchen table, his arms a-dangle and tingly numb (if he were aware), his forehead planted like rolling into a headstand, a stream of pooze draining from his nose onto the red formica, aggie eyes behind closed lids. Kid Jersey is what he calls himself. Kid Jersey is bruised, perplexed, hung-over, and nigh to expired in the heat. A motion of flies stirs above Kid Jersey's head, which is ordinarily affixed to a John B. Stetson pulled down to the eyes, but which has been tossed out the window of his Ford F-150 sometime during the night after catching the upchuck contents of his stomach. And there is blood spattered on his pointy boots. Perfect!

John Wayne shoot-em-ups is how it all began: five-year old Daryl squeezing Dad's hand at the pictures in Trenton, New Jersey, diminutive in the crease of the chair but red-leather fringed in matching vest and chaps, a silver-plated plastic Colt .45 clack! clacking! a white felt cowboy hat pulled snug. It was so clear back then what's bad and what's good. Town = Good. Prairie = Bad. Roy Rogers, The Lone Ranger, and Rin-Tin-Tin out there on the plains fighting Indians, busting rustlers, imposing acrobatics on gun slingers, those long gotcha! dead-falls off boulders and roof tops, receiving gracious thanks from smiling children and shop keepers, church goers waving hankies, and then a clatter of hooves back to prairie to start it all over again. Daryl sinks deep in the plush cushions of the family den, a bowl of vanilla melting on the arm rest, his mouth tense, his eyes overwide with dreaming, singing *Happy Trails*, riding high in the saddle, performing anonymous good deeds a-plenty, a wonder dog at his heels so loyal it could make Daryl cry. Daryl cries. Who was that masked man? Perfect!

But when religion asserted itself, induced in Daryl's pre-teens, it shifted his thinking -- all those loners of the Old Testament clept heroes, all those misfits and outcasts favored of Yahweh. Town = Bad. Prairie = Good. Sodom gets nuked! So why does God talk to Himself like He's multiples? Let *US* go down and confound their speech, God says, like He's been alone too long in the desert and it's addled His personality, not to mention His judgment. God is psycho. "No, Daryl, God is good. Prairie is good," Rabbi Cohen insisted. "Yes, believe me." Rabbi Cohen took significant numbers of Daryl's weekends for youth retreats to entrench his Jewishness, which eventually he began to see as his otherness, as perceived in stories of sacrifice and survival despite overwhelming odds, or maybe on account of it.

But all this just pushed him deeper into cowboy movies, the dark ones where the good guys are loners, drifters in expiation, marked for Cain in their exploits: like the David and Goliath showdown at Abraham Plains, for instance, the original face-off of good and evil. And David gone wrong when gone to town, because not only gone to town but become King of his people, presiding in the capital city, chasing married women and murdering their husbands. Daryl had begun to see that the little guy, the loner with ambition, raw courage and fast hands, he could win. In high school, one of those exclusive private schools, Daryl asserted himself into the quick of significance: become a captain of sport, a bookish brown-nose, disarmingly moderate as editor of his school's newspaper, an idol to giggly ordinarily unapproachable girls, first in his class to get layed behind the bleachers, spiffy in his dark-blue sport jacket with the embroidered school crest. He was Marshal Dillon with an agenda: securing main street is good for business; comforting Miss Kitty is comforting self. Chester Goode limps several paces behind calling his name. Chester never gets any. Rabbi Cohen is wrong. Town is good! if you're bad.

As if to hammer the point, what Daryl saw of the effects of town on a truly good cowboy, a humiliated favorite marquee hero, well -- the guys in the white hats, they simply collapsed, pillars of salt. This was in high school, still, with Daryl secretly, quietly harboring cowboy dreams. But they were to become for Daryl imposed realities inhabiting painted sunsets and cardboard towns, bit actors with alcohol problems and capped teeth and house mortgages. This realization landed with the authority of a repossessed future.

All because Dad thought he had contrived the perfect vacation: "Let's take the kids to Vegas!" That's what Dad had said, which is about as much wild-West as a New Jersey bond trader can think, figuring show girls and mafia and black jack -- that's about as real as it gets. So the family took Thanksgiving week and drove all the way out and back in their Volvo wagon to authenticate the experience, intersecting Rt. 66 whenever possible to give "the kids" a taste of that more recent migratory path that had replaced the Oregon Trail, each littered with encumbrances that hinder transit, the more recent being Tarot card readings, exotic animal petting zoos, all you can eat buffalo ribs, Indian powwows, bull fights and Elvis on black velvet. And once at Vegas, Dad drank to excess in the ghoulish whore gilt of Miss Kitty's saloon, loosened the belt on his tight ass and gambled away a tidy sum, the infection of free spirit having spilled over to Mom who pulled a one-armed bandit with abandon like jacking a lover while the kids got into the wet-bar booze upstairs where TV jangled day and night with Mom & Dad appearing infrequently to hassle room service. Finally, Mom came to her senses, or maybe had worn her own arm to a frazzle, and told the kids she'd take them to a show.

That's when one of Daryl's heroes took a tumble, dressed in black up there on stage, his hair a pouf of cock feathers dyed jet black, projecting a quavering voice and shaking belly at them like some Buddha ventriloquist -- Rusty. None other than RinTinTin's buddy, middle-aged and paunchy. And RinTinTin, youthful as ever, tricked-out in a rhinestone collar, doing silly dog tricks: "Yo ho, Rinty! Fetch the cigar, Rinty! No, no. Don't play with matches. I'll light the cigar myself. Good boy!" (the German shepherd sits upright patiently on its haunches, turns its head to face the audience, does a Milton Berle, perplexed and ironic, paws crossed at his chest -- big laughs!) "What's that, boy? (the dog whines) All right then, but don't inhale." Rinty inhales. What's about that? Wonder dog and doggy daddy go spangly and high-tonsuled in the corrupting saloons. Why'd you go to town, Rusty?

Daryl had to get some perspective on what he'd seen, once they had retraced their lane through the alkali desert, crossed the rim of a rather grand canyon, scudded through clouds over bald mountains and landed back in Jersey. He gave up on the Hollywood version and went straight to biographies of those he knew to be the real thing: Wyatt Earp, the Sundance Kid, Buffalo Bill. Real-life desperadoes and gun slingers of the old West. But they hailed from New Jersey and Ohio, or were dandies from Europe. Hell, to be a true cowboy you had to have been born in a teepee or under a rock in the Mojave Desert. This was terrible news. This was wonderful news.

Daryl had waited long enough. One early morning in the early spring of his senior year in high school, as dirty snow had begun to leak away into gutters, Daryl opened the garage door hours before Dad had addressed his sagging face in the shaving mirror. When Daryl turned the key in Dad's Porsche it barked its usual perkiness. He drove immediately into the hills of Pennsylvania, 95 per in the red glow of the dials, then beneath the St. Louis arch, and as the flatlands pulsed beneath his wheels, Kansas became a dream, and as he ascended the Grand Staircase, the Rockies snowed at him and specters in buffalo hide beckoned, which Daryl ignored. He was missed in AP English at Country Day Prep, missed later that day at Admissions of

Princeton University where he was meant to razzle-dazzle and secure a place in the freshmen class. He was not missed at home, however, as he had left Dad the Volkswagen Beetle to drive to work and so Dad figured the kid had taken the Porsche to better meld with the crowd of well-heeled Princetonites. Dad understood. Dad would buy the kid a new car soon anyway, maybe one of those MGB two-seaters, red, rollbar and convertible top. Daryl drove all through the day and night, day after day, shrinking noticeably emotionally and physically as the vast empty plains opened before him, a litter of fast food containers gathering in the back seat. He opened the throttle at the San Rafael Swell in Utah just as the sun declined. He found a used car lot twinkling beneath a halo of light bulbs on wires strung between telephone poles in the sleepy town of Delta and traded the Porsche for 500 pocket cash and a beat-up Ford truck. No paperwork.

Back on the highway, headed southwest through Cheyenne territory, he first paused at a truck stop off the I-6, where the burgers were cardboard and the coffee motor oil, but the smiles were genuine from gruff-and-well-tumbled waitresses with teased hair and rump dimples winking in tight jeans and from greasy-haired cowboys shaking still from the solid-weld chassis of their cattle-bearing PeterBuilts. The first thing Daryl asked: "Would you happen to have any work around here?" The waitress leaned on the counter, chewing gum in his face, speared the back of her ear with a pencil, said "shit" to that and looked four-square into Daryl's eyes. "How old?" she said, looking for a flinch. "Old enough to need a job," he said flinchlessly. "That's old enough," she said. "How many miles down the road worth of work you looking for?" she said. "Far enough so I don't have to change my name," he said, with a flush of accomplishment, that line simply falling out of the sky and into his lap, a gift from somewhere deep in Plato's viewing room, brought to life in the one place on earth where it belongs, which left the waitress unfazed except that she reached under the counter for a white apron, said "The coffee is comped, the burgers half priced and the kitchen thataway." He was the only one in recent years with his arms deep in the froth of a double-sink pot wash that didn't talk Spanish. He had French. Here was another life lesson, another practical application of a pricey education. Daryl tried out his best Clint Eastwood sneer and snake eyes -- he had the pale blue eyes, though his lips weren't maybe as thin as they should be. The taco boys seemed to be insisting that he clean the grease trap which had a gorge-rising stink. Daryl repeated his squinty eyes and off-putting smirk and planned on being left alone. Daryl got instead a beating in the freezer walk-in. Perfect.

Twenty dollars and change and another 1/2 priced burger later, he was back on the road with a full tank of gas, a bruised eye, and a noticeably wobbly back set of tires, which turned out to be the axle, which isn't a bad thing entirely if you drive the back roads (soft dirt more forgiving than tar macadam) and keep the speed down. These were valuable life lessons. He began to assess the character he wanted to project now that he was out where the free range ranges. He had to do more mean, outsider mean, reclaim himself out from the self-effacing void of deep horizon, cultivate a you-can't-domesticate-me kind of mean, which meant that women were out, in all ways conceivable -- lovers, mothers, friends. He could not allow himself to be drawn into community, at least not emotionally, which is what women are best at Daryl figured. As if to assert this new persona going deeper into mean, Daryl stomped the accelerator, fish-tailed onto soft shoulder, kicked up a blinding dust cloud, drifted farther into desert, kept the wheels turning fast so as to grip crust and gravel and bedrock now and again, leveling mesquite, and finally came to rest in a dry gulch that hadn't seen water anytime within recent memory, and that had probably got carved out by a flash flood sucked to aquifer almost immediately. The truck had its butt in the air like a dog in heat. Well, that's all right. Daryl was making this up as he goes anyway. Perfect.

He pulled his back pack out from the cargo box and set his feet in the direction of paved road that quivered like mercury in the distance, *Treasure of the Sierra Madre* hallucinatory, and him moseying directly into that haze like walking on water. The boots of soft calf skin he had bought at a mall in Hackensack, a spiffy pair of points with big heels, they hurt like hell. He was doing a marathon on his toes for Christ sake, squeezing them little piggies together so they wanted to squeal. Perfect.

He walked that road for two days, half-conscious and all knotted up in his joints, sweated in the daytime and chilled at night, entirely unaware that in the dusky hours of the second day a blue Datsun pick-up truck was gaining fast behind with chicken feathers flying in its wake. It passed him in fact, feathers shuddering on the thin air. The Datsun skidded far right to avoid him. Braked. Had a look-see. Daryl was still wobbly un-awares and ambling straight down the middle. It was the dog barking that brought him around, some mutt terrier with wiry snout hairs that had its head out the window of the passenger seat and got to braying at him like there was still enough life left in him to be bothered. There wasn't. He remembers trying to smile at someone soft spoken and kind who led him to the tailgate. When he tried to speak his lips split and bled. He sucked on them, his only libation since that oily coffee back at the truck stop. He lay in the back of the truck with crates of chickens and looked for a mo-ment at the merging stars in a sky so beautiful it could make you cry. He cried. Perfect.

He had been found by a rancher's young wife re-turning from the open market at Ely and heading for the small chicken ranch she shared with her husband, her young son, and the aforementioned dog. They were all as frustrated as their chickens, scratching deep to find sustenance in a played-out landscape. Even scorpions were unhappy in the rock-busting heat and cold and drought of the past couple years. To make matters worse, the bank was threatening to foreclose, the husband had taken to drink. Both mother and child were looking for a hero to ride in from off the desert. Perfect.

Once Daryl had been nursed back to health, a couple days of fever sponged away by the solicitous young wife, chicken broth and vaseline lips and all that, he got to work doing the hero thing: applying what he had learned in AP Economics to the family's hardships, he concocted a plan to borrow off their assets, which he had hyperbolized to get a reasonable rate, so as to expand their operation two-fold by raising a barn with heat lamps for chicks, so as to realize a profit within three years. Meanwhile the husband slept off a hangover. The young wife looked at Daryl with extreme tenderness. The boy got out a shoe box and gifted Daryl his most valuable rookie card, a dog-earned and mean-eyed Ty Cobb that had once belonged to Dad. Next day Daryl went into town with Dad who drank and slept in the passenger seat of the Datsun -- the little boy said, "Don't go into town, Daryl! They hate us there. Dad comes back all beat up." Daryl brought along his figures from off the scratch pad to the bank's loan officer, who shook his head and smiled through his objections, but Daryl stood behind his calculations and AP Economics preparation insisting that the loan officer bring his proposal to the bank president who chewed out the loan officer for overlooking the logic of numbers in favor of class prejudice (the loan officer's daddy being a cattle rancher). Daryl got the loan processed, which included a hefty cash advance for incidentals, left the paperwork in the truck, left Dad in the bar where he had sneaked off, pulled the dog out from the back end of the truck with a leash, stuffed the cash in his back pack and hired a tow truck to pull his F150 out from dry gulch and made off for Vegas. Perfect.

He drove those back roads into another night. It wasn't too far down the road to get to Vegas, he thought, because of the night-sky glow in the distance. He couldn't know the hills were simply discharging radiation. Daryl braked to give a ride to an old man from off the Reservation that had ambled into his headlights. He had a long, gray pony tail knotted to perfection, a face lined and scaly from the sun but heart-shaped with those beautiful Asian cheek bones. A pouch of beaded leather hung from a hand-tooled belt with a buckle large and oddly toad shaped, turquoise set in silver, a mirror of the desert sky at high noon. He said one word: "T-la-ték-ti." Which Daryl took to be a town somewhere down the road. Daryl said: "Sounds quaint, sounds authentic," Because that seemed the right thing to say. The Indian called himself Charlie Two Feathers and smiled two uppers spaced like fangs. His mouth closed again and his face went instantly rigid. The Indian looked straight ahead, cigar store wooden, and stayed that way for hours until suddenly gesturing officiously for Daryl to turn the vehicle onto faint paths through mesquite and cacti. Kid Jersey followed these gestures for another hour through the hard-packed, orange desert until the path ended at a faded blue trailer positioned equidistant from the butt-ends of a rock formation that, with the trailer adjoining, made a perfect triangle. The sun had by then become glow worm enough to expose features of that trailer emerging from shadow: he saw windows missing and a door swinging on its hinges, part of the roof ripped back from a violent wind. The thing seemed uninhabited and uninhabitable. "Is this abso-lutely where you live?" said the Kid. The Indian seemed to grunt affirmation. This was not exactly what Kid Jersey had in mind as authentic cowboy ex-perience, but it was for sure real in a way he had never experienced real before. "Tlaltechti," said the Indian once again, and "sipapu" when the truck had braked to a stop. He spread his arms to encompass the immedi-ate landscape and said again, "sipapu."

"So, we're here -- the Chickasaw burbs," said the Kid. Where he had arrived was the red man's place of emergence from the dark underworld, "sipapua," a place where life must be regulated, controlled, the mind free of evil, rituals performed in earnest and unpolluted of non-believers.

Charlie Two Feathers pulled out from his leather pouch a pipe and tobacco, tamped with a stained thumb the sweet leaf into the bowl, pulled out from his jeans a vial of white crystal and pinched a generous lump which he ground with his thumb and forefinger into the top of the bowl which he lit and toked and smiled a second time his gat teeth and passed the bowl to Daryl and opened the door extending one lanky leg.

"Hold up there, chief!" said Kid Jersey remembering a thousand unanswered questions, abandoning reservations.

But Charlie Two Feathers had already vacated the truck leaving behind the pipe with Daryl. There was nothing compelling Kid Jersey to go native, but he had seen enough of Indian ritual in the movies to know that smoking the clay pipe, or "cloud blower" as the Indians call it, would cement a relationship between the indigenous and the intruder that could be of benefit sometime later. He wondered if he'd wind up with his own Tonto in the bargain. He toked and held the harsh smoke in his lungs as long as he could before expelling all in a racking cough. He knew instantly he was in for a rush. It took seconds. First he puked, had the wherewithal to pull his hat off his head and retch in that. Then the view morphed into linking diamond panes that filtered the morning light, an insect he had failed to notice earlier upped the volume like turbine jets winging overhead, his body temperature rose several degrees leaving him limp and flushed but comfy as a babe in a bassinet, he began to feel himself intimate with desert rhythms (sand passing like years through his fingers, the scent of sage growing gardens in his brain, the ground teeming with animal life), a tide of well-being moved through his body. Daryl sat in the truck for another hour steeped in a pleasant after-glow.

When he stepped out from the truck, a bit woozy and disconnected still, the ground all silty pulled at his boots like a current. Daryl tried to call out to Charlie Two Feathers but his voice had shriveled to a whisper and even that got sucked into the desert sky. He heard the dog bark and noticed boot tracks leading to one of the orange outcrops of rock and followed, somehow got his feet and hands to grip the seams and pulled himself up over the top where, to Kid Jersey's amazement, a twinkling pond of water lay in a moiling green sand that he eventually understood to be an infestation of giant toads -- hundreds of them! Together they chirped a bass note that Daryl recognized as the insect noise that had droned in the cab of the truck during the apex of his buzz. And there was Charlie Two Feathers in their midst, his face yellow in a pollen wash, lifting toads, one after another, rubbing the backs of their necks with a red cloth, squeezing oils from that cloth into a small clay bowl, smiling and chanting. He frowned at Daryl and said, "Tlaltechti" and then "Sipapu." The dog hopped up and down on its front legs, barking merrily at the perimeter of this sea of toads. Daryl was confused. He felt betrayed, left for a zombie, introduced to a nightmare world. His throat swelled with loathing. He couldn't make words. Daryl fell to his knees among the toads, grabbed one by its hind flippers and dashed out its brains, rose to his feet and began to kick toads into the air with his pointy cowboy boots, toads flying all around, their fat belly sacks eviscerating, exploding.

Charlie Two Feathers shouted something Daryl couldn't make out and charged at him, beating Daryl on the face with two bony fists, more severe than Daryl would have thought possible, but more insulting than painful, given the Indian's vast years and willowy frame. Daryl began to strike back, knocking the Indian down many, many times, and Charlie Two Feathers going at Daryl again and again until his own face had become a pulp of watery tomato. He finally lay with the toads, who blanketed him as if aware their shaman were in trouble, while saying in a broken voice and in Indian speak that Daryl must not kill him, as should he cease to exist, so too his race and with that, Father Sky and Mother Earth.

So this is it, thought Daryl, the authentic cowboy experience. I've beat the shit out of my own Tonto. Perfect.

Daryl crawled back down the rock face and entered the trailer, found the pipe in his pocket and lit the bowl and toked and made the whole thing go away. He awoke in the morning heavy limbed and swollen in

the face like bee stung. The Indian was gone, his pick-
up truck was gone, even the dog was gone. He was left
with this tin-can shelter deep in never-land and a
spring infested with hallucinogenic toads. Not so perfect. A vision in need of revision. Maybe not enough
mean. Kid Jersey decides to try again.

He opts to keep the Carrera Porsche this time
and lays rubber west across wheat fields and over
mountain passes, the nation's eye-popping wonders
blinking in the Porsche's halogen lights, tunneling deep
into America's past. He stops only to replenish fuel,
takes out the Visa, which he has slipped from Dad's
wallet, and buys enough Drake's coffee cakes to fill the
back seat, and big-gulps of carbonation indifferently
flavored, and at one of those highway truck stops in
the desert that sells everything you might not have
remembered to pack, Daryl puts together an ensemble
in black of boot-leg jeans, a shiny cotton shirt with
scalloped pockets and pearl snaps, a Stetson hat, and
of course, a pair of silver boots. The Porsche is already black. He leaves behind in the bathroom, neatly
folded, his preppy khakis and school jacket. He had to
flush twice.

Kid Jersey has a near religious experience driving
into sunset but comes out the other side remarkably
unaffected. He drives into another day, through another night, crosses the Great Divide and by mid-day
sees far ahead in the shimmer of sun on roadside, a
looming figure in the shape of an **L** trekking the cen-

ter line. Kid Jersey guns the engine thinking to rip past whatsoever may intend to impede his progress, but reconsiders as the figure becomes a lone wobbly Indian with a mangy dog tethered on a leash. The Indian is old as dirt. Daryl down-shifts the Porsche, which emits a whiney protest, and brakes alongside the Indian who ignores Daryl, just keeps on keeping on, outpaces the Porsche with his indifferent shuffle in dusky deer-skin buskins and red-beaded jersey. Even the dog ignores Daryl who guns the Porsche's engine then slips it in gear and jumps ahead, hits the electric window and leans out his head in that Stetson like a prairie dog poking out its burrow.

"Howdy old timer. Where's the powwow?" says Kid Jersey.

"Fuck you, pale face," says the Indian. Even the dog curls its lip in a pathetic snarl.

Daryl is understandably stunned. He sits a moment disbelieving as the two doddering sojourners gain distance. Daryl goes squinty eyed, pops the clutch and stomps the accelerator -- 0 to 60 in minimal seconds. The dog effects an inconsequential lift of tires, a dull thud, becomes a grease spot. The Indian flings his finger in the air, universal salute among the races, and keeps it there as Daryl motors farther into desert.

Down the road aways he sees a blue Datsun pickup truck parked on the shoulder with its hood braced open, another universal sign. Daryl slows just enough to catch in his rear view mirror a fetching pair of buns in cut-off jeans long legs stretching and calf muscle flexing, a curvy torso leaning deep into an uncooperative engine. Kid Jersey locks the brakes, pivots on his seat for a better view, at which time the figure has turned to face the Porsche, long blonde hair all greasy now, a pink tank top all greasy now too, but fetching altogether as the frustrated fair sex, alluring as the desperate fair sex. Daryl slaps the shift into reverse and burns rubber all the way to the Datsun. The young lady sweeps back her hair, shimmering in a plume of steam. Daryl sees vexation distort an otherwise youthful and inviting face, a face more appropriate to unconcern. Daryl is immediately smitten, chivalrous.

"Howdy, Ma'am," Daryl says fumbling a hat tip. "Can I assist?"

"The fuckin' radiator. Leakin' all over Hell."

"Darn shame."

"I am about to tie off the hose with this here rag," she says brandishing said rag, "but I am so mad at Carl, that's my old man, the damn fool which I told that this thing was heatin' up, I am so stompin' mad can't get out the chute. Ever had a day like that, cowboy? I need a lift."

"Well heck yes, Ma'am" says Daryl to both the question and the imperative, still reveling in his first ever time having been clept "cowboy," basking in the after-glow.

"Let me git my things."

Her things amount to a six pack of Rolling Rock desert temperature and already sampled.

As Daryl's Porsche leaps back down the road and the back end of the Datsun goes raucous with crated chickens, the travelers take a long look at each other. Smiles bloom and eyes twinkle. She calls herself SuzyQ, says her chicken ranch is just five miles further, says her husband is weak, a drunk, she has discovered, unable to cope with an impatient bank to which they are several months in arrears obligated. She has a son that looks like *him* and whines like *him* and, well, you can imagine. She looks at Kid Jersey with liquid blue eyes inviting his embrace. They embrace. They are instantly a pair. As SuzyQ and Kid Jersey pass by the played-out and run-down chicken ranch (a tow head boy of maybe ten years scratching designs in the dirt, his stumbling father patching a roof with flattened tin cans), SuzyQ gives a drover's "whoop" and rips off her T-shirt and sails it out the sun roof. The tank-top shivers at the peak of its ascent and then shuffles sideways to & fro, a big pink leaf coming to rest near a pair of chickens that had got too close to the Porsche and exploded in the wheel wells.

SuzyQ's breasts are as cute as her upturned nose, all freckled and pink, flushed with joy. Kid Jersey can't be happier. Daryl notices that SuzyQ needs a bit of sartorial replenishing. He pulls in at a road house as the sun begins to set, the usual Thursday night band doing a tolerable warm-up jangle of a Dolly Parton tune. The lead singer dressed like a rodeo queen, chunky and blessed with a voice that goes all the way down but still finds its way back up and out. Daryl lays down the Visa, buys a medium touristo-T off the back wall behind the bar -- "Whoop it up at Busters!" is what it says in gold lamé and beneath that silhouettes in an embossed highway shield, a couple coupling with hats flagging like bronco busting, and further beneath the shield in that same golden script "Ride 'em cowboy!" SuzyQ likes it. She says, "Well, shoot, baby. We been whoopin' since before Busters. Let's you and me show 'em what's to whoop about." SuzyQ scrambles into the back seat of the Porsche, which is parked at the front entrance of the road house, people toing and froing, Suzy's short-shorts off by now, her pinkly warm and inviting self gesturing for Kid Jersey to join her. Which of course he must. And so he does, somewhat awkwardly. The leaf springs of that high performance car getting more test up and down than what the Teutons had intended, folks removing their wide brims to press noses against the tinted windows for a better look-see. Perfect.

By the time they make the town of Little Whiskey, one traffic light at the only crossroads for miles, a lone pulse of color to contest the dark, even the police station has closed for the night. Daryl swings the Porsche around past the only bank, runs the light with a clean conscience, accelerates in the direction SuzyQ says he'll find a motel, locks the brakes just as quick as the darn thing is right behind the bank. It's the motel where SuzyQ lost her virginity back in high school with the gym teacher, the one where the town's only whore takes her johnnies, the one that's been lit at night off a faulty gasoline generator for years (the owner's resolve in a dispute over a utility bill), so it's bright as a prison break one minute and black as pitch the next. The net effect is a beacon for the disaffected, the wander-weeds, the discontented, the bottle floo-zies, the seriously disconnected, not to mention the not-so-secret lovers ten degrees off the bead of someone's shotgun sights.

They take a room, and moments after flicking on the light, an ersatz Elvis table lamp replete with guitar and lip twitch (a switch at the base will emit one grind-ing hip swivel, if they had bothered), SuzyQ has her T-shirt off again and they are going at it on the bed with magic fingers vibrating beneath. Daryl gets out a vial of white powder. SuzyQ says, "Goody!" And they snuffle from a rolled dollar bill like piggies rooting in soil. They exaggerate their happiness, they screw again, they drink from the remains of SuzyQ's Rolling Rock six pack already down to four. SuzyQ suggests they check out the bar that had years beyond her memory appended itself to the butt-end of the motel like a blind dog humping in the night. It is the only place in town to quaff a beer and spin a slow dance off a juke. When the two of them walk in arm in arm, runaway smiles on their faces, the habitual patrons, all leaning and stooping and scraping like gravity has increased in that bar beyond Earth tolerances, they all take offense all at once. Besides these anonymous extras, there is roadhouse Buster sharing with the bartender, in his upset, a certain performance of randy nakedness at the customer entrance of his establishment. He has come to the town of Little Whiskey to unwind and maybe hit on the town's only whore. And there is an Apache shaman seated on a stool end of the bar, a dusky and ancient specimen, holding a leash that trails to the floor from which dangles a bloody, furry ear. He has come to drink a parting libation to kachinas, an ancestral spirit from the snowy mountains having recently been splattered back to spirit. There is too a very drunk and abandoned husband definitely hitting on the town whore with a shot gun leaning beside him in a booth. Kid Jersey reaches for his guns, but they're back in Jersey, in a toy box somewhere in his bedroom closet. SuzyQ withdraws her arm from Daryl's and takes three steps back. But it doesn't matter. She is in this too. The little boy who had been sleeping in the Datsun pick-up truck is rapping with his tiny fists on the window saying, "You shouldn't of come to town, Ma! You shouldn't of come!"

The several assorted usuals that have been frequenting the only bar at Little Whiskey for years waiting for something to happen, something so big it will plug them into the myth of the American West that has so far excluded them, they are only too eager to participate. SuzyQ gets raped that night by a bunch of very appreciative drunks turned vigilante, and Daryl gets beat to shit, run out of town with a shot gun. The only useful thing he manages to do on his tearful and bloody path out the door is kick in the face of that little boy that had come at him with tiny fists. Daryl ruins his boots on that kid's face. Daryl drives ninety-per into the desert night, one eye closed up with swelling, the road morphing from macadam to desert sand, his stomach constricting then launching contents into the Stetson he manages to pull off his head in time and nearly fills, then skidding in a slippery mess of migrating toads that have got beneath the wheels, and landing his Porsche ass-up in a dry gulch. Perfect.

Kid Jersey walks aimlessly beneath the desert stars, down a dirt path with cacti looming like old testament giants. He eventually comes to a rock cliff which has giant toads leaping off like lemmings, and there at the base of these rocks sits the shell of a mobile home. Daryl walks in unannounced, finds a table and chair and lays his head down to rest. He will go back to town again soon. This is far from over. Perfect.

Penguins

Penguins walk funny. It is the wings. They take no purchase in the thin air. They hang limp as plant fronds. Penguins have forgotten what wings are. They don't care we think they don't know what to do with their wings. They are what they are. They have exchanged wings for flippers, changed their domain with their forgetfulness. I admire penguins. To be so steady in their wobbles, so unassuming beneath the sky and graceful among the fishes. If only we could find an element from which to issue grace. Because we're Godawful clumsy on land. And we die in water. Maybe we should just not care what people think about us. Maybe we should drown ourselves.

Orin Wobbleduster was not graceful on land. I know. I

was his mailman. I mis-delivered a letter that inspired him to take his life. I am on the road off my accustomed route, a load of orphan mail steeped in the back of my Jeep. I am not in the mood. I do not give a shit about customers anymore. I find them all despicable. I am driving north to consort with penguins.

What Orin was looking for in his mailbox was a cash settlement on a right-of-way he had been contesting in Orange County Court for two years. Some flatlander that plays banjo wanted to build a banjo-playing porch squat upon a tiny slice of land some neighbor of Orin's had sold to said flatlander. His greasy handshake moved town fathers to apportion the best deal possible in contravening environment specs and power-line access. Said flatlander had used Orin's property to access the site upon which arose the house he built. It was only just a seasonal access. Deeded there by a more generous town fathering for any long-time-ago farmer that tilled the land back of Orin's land and needed a way over to plant and harvest. Said flatlander thought to play Orin for that skinny bit of seasonal admittance, price it into permanence. Orin wouldn't have it. "The season for building is ended," he said. Said flatlander protested. Orin said back: "Build yourself a heliport."

Do you know that flatlander had the cheek to march into Orin's house next day unwelcomed, traipse straight to the kitchen, said, "Look, Orin, I'll give you enough money to build a real kitchen. Plumbing and cabinets and marble counter tops. Maybe an island with butcher block? Would you like that, Orin? A nice fat check. Let's say five thousand." Then he left. That was all Orin needed to oppose this man to the grave. I delivered that $5,000 check to Orin's tilted lidless mailbox, placed it deep inside to avoid wet from melting snow at the opening where sunlight gathers. Next day I delivered said check unopened in its envelope back to the PO inscribed "return to sender." This is not the letter I miss-delivered.

Of course, after Orin's day in court, the town picked sides. That's what got me involved. I ran through so much gas idling my Jeep beside boxes with customers discussing the Orin predicament that OPEC has assessed me fleet status. That's exaggeration, but you get the point. About this town, I should explain. It is a mountain village with twenty houses around a lake, a picturesque floating bridge a hundred years old that sells postcards. The bridge was once just wood planks across ice to unite two sides of the town: general store, Post Office and Inn on one side; farmers the other. One of those farmers, too lazy to hitch and prod his dray horse the long way round Pond Road, he drowned, the horse too, when his ride lost footing and broke the ice, so planks went down to keep the next farmer dry which were found to float when ice melted which gave town fathers an idea to make it suitable to horse and buggy year-round. These days it is a single lane of planks on barrels that leaf-peeping SUV's rumble across ignorant of risk. The sign says: 2,000 LB. LIMIT, TRUCKS AND FARM EQUIPMENT PROHIBITED.

I set in the Jeep sometimes with lunch and watch bridge people that fish daily off the sides and challenge passing cars to splash them from the water that seeps up from wood slats so they can fling foul words or errant fists if it comes to that. Sometimes they bring lawn chairs. I saw one guy fling an aluminum chair at a car. And the language is sometimes awful purple. But you have to understand. Cussing buoys the powerless. It is them that is most willing to go deepest in their insults to the hurt that evades expiation. The preacher of our Pond Church told me this. Bridge people drive junkers and park up the hill to pop clutches for a jump start. They come here from Granite Town down the valley where police hassle their behavior which we mountain townies put up with because our one constable is only part-time and most of that time chasing stray dogs. The ones not set afire. I will speak more of this later. The forest ranger does most of the arrests up here. He is the only one carries a gun with a permit.

Anyway, I am setting there squeezing tuna fish slippery

in mayonnaise into my lap from between slices of white bread. I am anticipating penguins. It could happen. Stranger things happen. When this New Jersey Cadillac Escalade, white and shiny with beige leather seats, rumbles across boards toward me parked opposite end of the bridge, the farmers' side of the lake, when the woman driving slips off the double slats that have been lain as a track to withstand wear. There is a discernable thump and some slippage of tires in green moss. She panics. Slams the brakes which skids her vehicle up against skinny protective rails, the ones bridge people lean on to fish. She has got these wide, scared eyes. Her SUV has come to a stop bulging out those rails. She is very near going over. I am wondering should I go in to save her? Dive where the fishes play, where the penguins glide gracefully, deep among cast-away beer bottles and the nightmares of midnight skinny dippers that leap into the black pretending fearlessness. I dismount the Jeep, purchase her attention with a motion of hands suggesting discretion in her maneuvers. She looks at me with hate, which under these circumstances I have some trouble interpreting. But, yes, it is hate. She cranks the wheel of her SUV away from said rails and accelerates. Two rails and a post split and drop into water. Her SUV somehow rights itself and skids toward me. I leap away. She thunders up the hill with a middle finger in the air. I do not get people. I really do not. Would penguins act that way? What, I wonder, is unacceptable behavior among penguins? What is community among humans except a way to organize and express our dislikes? It is basic to our nature. We dislike so many things.

The town's early days placed it on the stage line from Boston to Montreal. So despite its isolation, there has always been an Inn with pub gatherings. Several have gone up and burned down since the colonials. There is always a party in town. Now it is middle-aged hippies roasting pigs and giving "theme" parties to celebrate surviving these snowed-in-winters on trust funds, some on a knack for subsistence living. The highway these days bypasses town, can only be heard, not seen, somewhere above the tree line, the next ridge over, where eighteen wheelers rumble to Montreal. The main road through town is still dirt. Which is picturesque to tourists and a pain in the ass to anyone that lives here. The Inn is now run by a woman so grating of personality that I can not think anyone but relatives rent those rooms. The Inn's business has subsided a good deal. The owner hides in there somewhere with the radio on, some station of French Canada. There is a B&B run by our resident witch for which there is evidence. Her husband tinkers the house occasionally but mostly takes long naps. He used to contract house building but now no one lets him. His last effort, a poured foundation facing the wrong way, crumbles frost-heaved and tree-root shifted. There is a New York City cartoonist that cashed-in on a nose fetish (he is our mayor un-elect, which you find out if ever you barrel burn garbage and get a phone call from our only constable telling you of the fine our mayor un-elect has levied you). There is a family from Canada, an investor banker that parties with the hippies and has two young sons inclined to animal torture: pets disappear then wail through town dead of night their backsides ablaze. This I have mentioned earlier. And there is a man from Boston lives alone beside the lake in the old pitchfork factory that hates everybody except stray dogs. He feeds the ones that survive scorching. Somehow he is the only human in town any of them will trust, maybe because he is dying of cancer, but if that is so, it is the slowest cancer I know. Too slow for some. I deliver him packages of miracle cures from Mexico. He has threatened the lives of our animal immolators. We all respect him for this. We all wonder when his house will catch fire. There is a small restaurant that caters to the Inn with red haired kids flooding the school system and raucous weddings which the bridge people crash. And there is a real estate agent that has had a hand in the Orin Wobbleduster suicide.

This real estate agent is so smart he overestimates himself and underestimates everyone else. He thinks Orin has not evolved beyond fungus. Which might not be too far a reach to see Orin's farm house that sets above the village near the highway shimmering in steel-blue moss laced with years of flinty road dirt. Orin is the last Wobbleduster to work the farm, "work" being a customary term that does not necessarily always translate as "work" per se. What Orin does -- he milks cows and throws dead cats into a shed filled with barking dogs of no discernible breed. These cats have multiplied like puffs of milkweed tossed by the wind. They live short lives and die indiscriminately from disease and vehicular incidence. I have killed a few myself getting to the mailbox. They lie in the road for days, dry out and flatten out, then disappear. Cat jerky for the pups.

What I am saying is Orin's place looks too care-worn to be comfortable for anyone but a cave bear, which is what Chad Drueplet says, and which Orin decidedly was not, although he had a furtive side. The pale blue of his eyes ranged beyond the nonsense people talk. Orin was known for looking around or above, as if nowhere in synch with the conversation, as if dodging it, then an undentured smile and a scrap of comment that shows he has been listening and thinking on two planes. His voice was almost too quiet to hear (don't ever call Orin on the phone, if it were not already too late): "Mostly upside down leaves come down the creek today. Could be a early winter. Get that extra cord of wood, Molly. Make that Inn keeper pay on the barrel for those eggs." That was Orin addressing a particular complaint of Chad Drupelet's wife. Orin had listened in his dodgy way for ten minutes, then made a single statement and walked away. Usually Orin kept to himself. I delivered a lot of magazines in black plastic. Orin had a bevy of glossy-paged lady friends. He got little action beyond his own self-interest or maybe a favorite cow or two. His toothless grin and off-putting breath were said to yellow magazine pages and scatter a herd of Jerseys. What I am on the way to saying is that Orin looked like he needed money bad. But he did not. Not until that banjo player wanted to pay him some. But I will get to this later.

At the time of the disruption of the banjo player, Orin had been given notice that the town was upset at his delay in back taxes. Of course this was a one-hundred-forty year delinquency in taxes. Orin did not give a shit about taxes. Neither did his family from the days the patriarchal Orin marched off to fight Johnny Reb. There have been Orins in every generation of Wob-bledusters since. The present Orin figured he was great-grandfathered out of taxes. His kin had not paid taxes since the eighteen sixties when survivors of the Civil War had returned to farms fallow and bereft of animal husbandry from pure neglect. Taxes were re-scinded to get those boys back on their feet. Orin's great grandfather stayed off his feet, smoked tobacco on the porch, told war stories, grew cats in the barn and burdocks in the fields. His farm has stayed the same since. Except now cats grow in the fields and dogs in the barn. But the introduction of the banjo player, in collusion with the real estate agent, pressured town fathers to spiff up the Wobbleduster property. If for no other reason than maybe the town could absorb said property for back taxes and parcel off the land to other well-intentioned, well-heeled flatlanders with flatlander architects to frame the view of floating bridge for leisure porches and bay windows. Big houses and big taxes.

Orin represented himself in court. The banjo player brought an attorney from the state capital that had recently warranted the lieutenant governor's confiscating five hundred acres in private property at bargain prices for a highway bypass which then gave the airport a go-ahead to move a trailer park for an expanded runway. Orin rolled into district court on his John Deere tractor. It was early spring, sugar snow in the air, the dirt roads rubbery with partial thaw, except for sections that bubbled with underground springs. I have lost the front end of my Jeep down a few of these when it was too early to know what was going on beneath. The town Orin came to has identical bandstand greens and is lately notorious for teenagers that cross state lines to rob and murder college professors at an ivy league college built for Indians that has long ago not gave a shit about Indians anymore, the ones that are left. And yes, these high school kids believe they come to the warpath through legitimate Indian bloodlines. College teachers should circle wagons. This town would seem to be perfect for a county court house. When Orin entered the courtroom, he was already a half hour late. Which was pretty good for Orin. The banjo player agitated over this, however, as billable hours were mounting. Orin greeted the judge with deference, his voice rising just above the sound of scratching scabs. "Your honor," he offered Drusala Purvis, a long, tall, dark haired lady with a suppressed sense of humor that could not be counted on to obey her better instincts in this situation – which situation was that Orin had farted voluminously when bending to remove his mud-clogged boots at the back of the courthouse while greeting Judge Purvis. This was not a dry, sneaked-out-the sphincter fart. This was a wet, carnival-barker.

Judge Purvis anticipated judiciously the apology that would follow said eruption but waited without result. There was, however, a smatter of giggles from citizens readied upon the docket of misfortune's wheel. And there were winces of disgust from the banjo player, his attorney, and his wife – a delicious, well-trimmed bundle of L.L. Bean catalogue wear. The judge, she held as long as she could then broke into toothy fits of laughter that stopped Orin's defrocking and mud scraping. Orin had got down past the crusty buttons of his hunting jacket and was about to strip off his workman's bib and overalls. The braces dangled by his knee when the judge reasserted her composure.

"Mr. Wobbleduster," she said in a rehearsed octave appropriate to the occasion.

"Judge?" he said back.

"Would you care to sit yourself upon the bench of the plaintiff?" said she. "You may hang your outerwear on the pegs outside these doors which you have entered so ceremoniously."

"No ceremony to it, Ma'am," said Orin. "I have come a long way here on my tractor which has taken some doing in the spring of our weather and I need to get back by afternoon for milking if we can do this quick and get my land back to me where it belongs and send this banjo fellow wherever he must go to get a heliport permit which should not be a hardship for him except that my livestock might not like the noise of the blades hovering but that I guess that is better than him taking from me a slice of property that has been in my family since great-grandfather shot him enough Johnny Rebs to consume his hours thereafter recalling and contemplating the warp and the weft of it all."

 The room nearly fell into the middle of itself leaning into the compact patter of Orin's words.

Orin's was the longest unsworn testimony ever allowed in that court. Judge Purvis saw to that. And that was

the longest string of words Orin had ever put together. But he had had a couple hours hugging together his body warmth upon that tractor from which
to contemplate and compose. However, it was the
Judge's sad duty to inform that Orin had not done
anything he was supposed to do to secure this strip of
property in question since the banjo player had begun
to hammer together a home. The judge besides had
taken the initiative to consult Orin's hometown by
which she discovered Orin's one-hundred-forty year
tax evasion. She did the right thing, most would say:
she gave that right-of-way to the banjo player at a very
high cost and set Orin's tax debt at the very same price
with the additional condition that Orin must pay that
tax bill by the first of the following month or lose
house and lands to the town. Coincidentally, the banjo
player must pay Orin for the right-of-way exactly one
week before Orin's taxes fall due.

The mail route brimmed with rumor. Drum beats in
the woods, smoke signals high upon the buttes, a
mailman leaning out the window of a right-hand-drive
Jeep -- same difference. Words passed from them to
me and down the line to more them waiting beside
their boxes for words further up the line. I never gave
my own thoughts. I prefaced what I said with "these
are not my thoughts." But it did not matter. I was
never consulted for my own thoughts. I was a conduit
only, a government agent of news.

The nosy cartoonist, his skinny bald self, leaned on his box, it was a pretty spring day, mud on the roads in the woods but drying considerable where the sun got to it. He said, "What's he thinking? That Orin? He should know better than oppose the laws. We all have rules to live by. We would be a society of fools with no recourse to reform foolishness if there weren't consequences to our actions. Orin needs to realize the consequences of his actions."

"These are not my thoughts," I said, but surely, you are right." I handed over the mail. The cartoonist removed his baseball cap, wiped his forehead with an agitated forearm, stuffed his box with the mail I handed him. He had just got back from an exercise run and apart from word of Orin's fate, wanted no part of what the outside world cared to impart.

"What's the B&B got to say about this?"

He always wants to know what the town witch thinks. He is the one caught her incanting in the back yard. Candles and pentagrams, her waxy voice and Latinate nonsense. It was about as spooky as this town gets is what he told me.

"These are not my thoughts, you understand, but you might need to live here a little longer," is what I said to that.

Some part of his rational mind niggles the witchy idea in discomfort, perhaps assailed by dogs wailing down main street at night, set afire and streaking toward the lake. The smell is god awful. It lingers for days. I can smell it on the pitchfork factory occupant each time I hand him his cancer cures. Donna Treehorn, the B&B owner, she says it is the stink of the devil.

Donna Treehorn waited by her box, disgust twisting her face. She said, "That banjo playing son of a bitch has got nerve. He came around here with his smooth face poked out his collar and aimed at me. I told him go where folks are too stupid to know what he's buttering. Of course he wants my consideration for taking Orin's land, for taking whatever he wants seems to me. I don't carry much love for Orin. But Orin has never taken anything from me I can't spare to give. Pity mostly. That banjo man better be careful what he buys that can't be returned."

It did not go down too good when I told Orin's neighbor, Chad Drupelet, what our unelected mayor had said. Chad hated Orin because they grew up together. He hates the cartoonist more because they did not. Chad said, "Why can't town business stay in town and us farmers take care of our own? I could make small work of Orin's problem with a bear bait perfume that would give that banjo player a visitation of dark

fur to chase him all the way back to paved sidewalks."
Chad lives off trapping bear. He tours the back roads
in a tin truck of Japanese make with beagles in the box
in a kennel with holes for barking heads.

What my customers were most curious about is Orin's
judgment of Judge Purvis's decision. Orin had told the
Judge to find work where she knew something about
the people she was deciding over. He said he was
keeping his land no matter. She thought she had decided the perfect solution. Orin wants to keep his
farm, the banjo player wants to buy the right-of-way,
the town wants its tax money. What they did not count
on was the degree of Orin's neighbor's hostility and
Orin's obstinacy in refusing to let go any tab of property to either the banjo player or the town. And of
course, my stupid mistake set wheels in motion.

When I miss-delivered Orin's check from the banjo
player, the second one, the one Judge Purvis ordered
to pay for the right-of-way, Chad Drupelet receives
and burns said check in his wood stove. This is what
he does with all miss-delivered mail. The town wants
money for back taxes. It knows the banjo player has
paid up. Orin says he don't have the check. No one
but Chad believes him. The town makes plans to auction off Orin's goods and confiscate his property. Orin
releases his dogs, which make a chaos of things for a
while: howling and mauling each other and the occa-

sional pampered lap dog in celebration of their inexperienced freedom, chasing bridge people into their cars, chasing the mailman. Some of them expire lit like torches at night and running through town, the scent of burned skin, fur and lighter fluid. The cats become more brazen. They copulate in a plague of domination and make a fur collar that encircles that farm and tightens its grip until nothing else can breathe. The cartoonist calls it "as bad as the cats in Rome." Can't say I follow. Orin cranks to a sputtering start his hay bailer and throws himself in. He is mauled into a tidy square of guts, twine and straw. It is discovered that he has kept a hefty life insurance policy, which pays off back taxes, and left a will that appoints Chad Drupelet caretaker of said property until Orin's heir can be located. Chad has no intention of finding said heir. He immediately goes about scenting the property to attract black bear, which leads the banjo player to rehire his lawyer, which leads Chad to fell a tree denying the banjo player use of the right-of-way to his home, which leads to another law suit, and another claim by the town that further back taxes are owed. All wind up back in court. Chad defends himself, of course. He brings to court and parks outside the front doors the blood-stained square baler with Orin's guts splashed on it. Judge Purvis has had enough: she sends everyone outside and back to their homes and offices with admonishments to just "get along" and leave her and the courts alone!

But this is not the end of the story. Yes, Chad assumes guardianship of the land. He provides for the cats as a kind of truce between them and his beagles. He fathers more towhead kids off Molly, a Quebec stripper he moved south to make an honest woman of. And I keep driving north. The reason is I am become a known victim of a cuckoo. That is another kind of bird less rare here than a penguin but not so nice. I have had Orin's kid in my nest for ten years. It was not until my wife, my two-hundred-pound honey (her skin is smooth as butter; I would not want any less of her), she tells me it is not Chad Drupelet's land. It is hers! She wants to go to court. That is how she said it. It is *her* land, but she meant it is Kitten's land. Kitten is our ten-year-old daughter. Seems appropriate a kitten would be taking over the land. But I had to ask myself, well, no, I had to ask Belinda (that is my wife). I had to ask her how it was Kitten would have Orin's property? She said, "Toby, Kitten is Orin's kid." She said it in a very understated way. I asked her to repeat what she had said. I asked her twice. I keep coming back to the penguins. What would a penguin have done? I mean, here is a situation that puts a man in about as awkward a position as possible. I felt out of my element. Nothing I could do would make me feel less awkward. But there was no water around, so I just plunged ahead: "Belinda, darling, baby, these are not my thoughts, but what you say does not make sense. I find I just can not believe you."

Her answer settled the matter. She said, "Toby, you're a fool."

Then she walked away. She took Kitten, she took everything in the bank account, she took the dog that still has its fur, she took the phone number to a lawyer friend who sent me in the mail, because he is my friend too, he sent me a xerox that said, "Kevin [that is the lawyer's name]," it said, "Kevin, tell my husband, Why's he think the dog got so damn friendly to Orin that it wagged its behind like about to rotate off its hips? Why's he think that dog and me took so many walks up around Pond Road? Why's he think Kitten looks so much like Orin? and I can hear him say what's that?" she said in the letter, "I can hear him, and the what's that of the what's that is that when she was born she had no teeth and no hair exactly like Orin. She may have grown out of Orin's looks with time but she started with them. I will be living on that property from soon to now on and I expect Toby to keep a distance. And tell him don't deliver me no mail. I will be taking a rented box in the neighboring town."

This is the story of a very real town that you will maybe locate but whose people I have given cameo names so I can not be sued and taken to Judge Purvis on account. Besides that I am still traveling north with nothing worth claiming damages off except maybe some checks in these mailbags I could cash because I do not intend ever to deliver them. I never could get the right mail to the right people. And besides, I have sworn off people. I am looking to join a colony of penguins. If you want to know my thoughts, I just want to live among the fucking penguins if you don't mind.

Lucius Ascending

I write for low-budget TV sitcoms mostly. Wholesome family values schlock, warmedies, the stuff that airs on the early fringe. My specialty is boomerang parents. They snowbird back home from Florida, gloomy with pension shock, sunburned from poolside bingo, trading their golf carts for Buicks, disenchanted with the Disney retirement plan. They return north to Buffalo and Milwaukee and Detroit carrying guilt like luggage into their kids' houses. They rearrange furniture, nail embarrassing baby photos to the walls, misguide the grandchildren, niggle and wit themselves into loveable dry sticks – "ha, ha" says the laugh track, very cute. But that's before cataracts and arthritis set in for real. We have to create new shows before the used-up loveable ones die on us. We make like in the real world mom and dad don't get packed off to the mumbling farm the minute they forget how to balance a check book.

My agent says the work has aged me, which means he sees residuals drying up along with my own advancing decrepitude. His pencil lingers more, scratches the ledger less. Bed-hopping twenty-somethings have cornered the market. Old people are not very sexy. He finagles the networks for repeat airtime to pay down the mortgage on his retirement villa in Cancun. My body has gone to hell -- fingers yellowed from nicotine, blood anemic. But when my heart throws arrhythmia up the doctor's stethoscope, that's me dancing a reel with the devil down the arterial corridors. I've struck a bargain for a friend.

Before I got the news my heart is a time bomb, before I heaved my cell phone into the pool, I made two calls -- one to enlighten my agent of a pending black-tie affair in memorial of me, and one to remind a well-connected Nashville recording studio executive about a favor he owes. I've rented a room in this run-down bungalow in Pasadena where I sit by the radio with the lights off and blow cigarette smoke out the Spanish grate that secures the window. It's been days. I'm listening to country music on WKBY, where my executive friend has a controlling interest. I'm anticipating a Johnny Cash debut tune of a Fenneman original with the usual mouthful of teeth rearranged by the boot-heel of life, but somehow hopeful. The studio exec knows Johnny Cash "with embarrassing intimacy," is what he said. Johnny has promised to cut a song that Lucius Fenneman wrote. Lucius is a nobody except to me. I don't know if Johnny likes the song or not. But that's not the point. He'll do it. I imagine Lucius sitting here beside me smiling, playing sweetly on his Martin acoustic, Johnny's whisky voice singing his words.

I met Lucius Fenneman in the 60's. I was in my twenties then, broke and jobless, trying not to look too hard at myself, avoiding the nostril shot as we say in the business. I had done a tour in Nam and was numb still. I had flown direct from Saigon to Los Angeles and had taken a cabby's advice to locate beyond the centrifugal mayhem of L.A.'s cloverleaves. I'd never been to L.A. but heard good things about the weather. I took a room in a single story tenement of cement block with yellow stucco chunking off and a flat roof. No trim. Built on a narrow plot, more long than wide, rooms arranged shot-gun off a single hallway like a bowling alley with a kitchen at the far end and a bathroom in the middle close to my room. "Pleasant housing in shared living environment with amenities, $25 a week" is what the ad said.

I got my hair trimmed G.I. by some American Legion barber with the shakes, a twisted character out of Andy Griffith who had taped *TIME* covers of Nam atrocities to the walls which he laughed about. I asked for a deep trim. He smiled, switched on the razor, left me a fuzzy bedpost with nicks. That's okay. I like to hear the wind whistle past my ears. The way I looked, could have been going back to Nam, which is what I had in mind if this experiment in civilian life hadn't taken hold. I needed this apartment. I needed four walls away from everyone I knew that wouldn't know me anymore. I had to look like I could pay the rent, like I could at least afford a haircut. As it turned out, I got the place easy enough, though I had to pay a three month advance, half my cash reserve, because I was under sixty-five so couldn't fall back on Social Security.

Wedged like a comma between Kentucky Fried Chicken open 24 hours and a tire warehouse, the place had grease-vat aroma all night and from 7 a.m. to 5 p.m. the sound of air guns loosening lug nuts. These must have been the "amenities." But it also had a tiny garden near the bathroom window that some crone had been tending on our side of the stockade fence with wisteria climbing that hummingbirds visited. But it's the bathroom with its busted window and urine smell and some other distinctly septuagenarian odors where this story begins.

"I'm Lucius. The girls call me Luscious, he said" -- I saw that coming -- "but you can call me Loquacious." Didn't see that coming. I didn't even know the word back then. I was also pretty cranky because no one had mentioned that in the rainy season, which it was at the time, a 1/4 inch of water would drain onto my floor at night from holes in a vertical pipe suspended in the center of the room. It looked like a catalytic converter on a VW and was supposed to radiate heat. On my first night there I had set a pair of Japanese sandals beside the bed. When the tire warehouse began to torque blue smoke not more than twenty feet from my head, I launched into the closet thinking bunkers and mortar fire. I hugged my knees, water lapping at my nads, and squirmed into the shadows until my breathing slowed. I felt stupid. My sandals were bobbing waves like a day at the beach.

I worked at night, six hours hawking subscriptions to the *LA Times* by phone. The crew there were mostly retired traveling salesmen, cynical and suspicious of youth, scraping for that 5% commission like it was a king's ransom. There was nothing but old people in my life even then. But I fit right in. My past played vivid and loopy, a chromatic nightmare, same as them. My future was a black & white photo in solution that refused to develop. After work I'd wander that tenement hall for hours past the blue TV screens and coughing fits of my neighbors, shoulders pitched forward as if humping a pack in the bush of Nam, working off the idiot energy of civilian disquiet.

I was lucky to have the communal bathroom and not the kitchen across from my room. Better to avoid the noise of bickering over missing leftovers and dirty utensils. Although how they knew whose box of KFC chicken parts was whose is beyond me. Better to know when the facilities were free, and pretty easy with those thin doors to monitor patterns of use. Old folks are "regular" in their bathroom habits. They stock Metamucil on the kitchen shelves. Probably use it as meat tenderizer. Twenty minutes after meals was the best time for me to avoid bathroom use -- a real stampede. Other openings were claimed by those on time-release medication, while twenty minutes before meals was my time. At least until I met Lucius.

Lucius Fenneman never did lock down a routine of throne visitation. He was the only one of us, me included, who didn't. So one morning when I had suffered as much pneumatic torquing as I could take and was straining in my jammies for that twenty minute pre-breakfast opening, I poked my head out the door and felt pretty sure the herd was focused on *Good Morning America*, loony tunes, miracle hands spirituals and Big Bird. No one would see me in the blue velour jumpsuit my stepmother had sent gift wrapped from Montgomery Ward when she heard I had come to L.A. The suit wasn't my style, but she thought it was L.A. personified, and it slept comfy. That's when I stepped in on Lucius all bruised and naked and crumpled and vomited on in the shower. The water wasn't running, which is why I didn't know he was there.

His limbs were tattooed in places, as was his chest, and flesh hung loose like it had been steamed off the bone. But there were plenty of flaps and folds to show that he had once taken a firm grip of the world and held tight.

"My God! What's that you're wearing, boy? The celestial blue angels have come for me!"

What?"

"I can see you're no stranger to rare sights, boy.

Wait till you see me up close. Only thing left of my youth is the sometimes zits I get on my shoulders. Had a dizzy spell. Couldn't find the handles to spin the water on. Think it was the hummingbird that's flitting out there on the vine outside this broke window. One good thing about the maintenance here -- they never do fix nothing."

When I helped him up, Lucius whizzed pink against the rusted shower stall and asked me to crank the handle to wash off the mess. The scent got punky with steam rising off the fermented waste of his stomach. It overwhelmed me. I took a seat on the porcelain.

"Sudden illness and accidents brings strangers together," Lucius said. "War is both. Ain't it, boy? You made friends in the bush. Am I right? Ain't so easy now is it. Think it was the wings that got me – the hummingbird. How its life must be over in a month to move so fast. It makes me sad. Temporary beauty. You know."

I knew that in about five minutes one of our punctual residents would be needing the facilities and would get panicky and flustered if not accommodated. So I helped gather Lucius off the metal basin and dried him. And that's when he started to sing a tune that I can still hear and that chokes me up as I think of it. His voice was hollow and whispery. The song had the usual country bluesy subtext but somehow ripped at the gristle and bone beneath the fat that had been criscoed onto my nerves to insulate or otherwise spare me of feelings. This he laid on me while I was trying to stay distant, drape his clothes on, drag him into his room and dial nine-eleven. I had been planning a breakfast of cold poptarts -- they're good doughy -- and a hike into the foothills of the Sierras. Maybe find a tree to sleep beneath. I found myself thinking out loud, telling Lucius about another time sleeping under a bausor tree in Nam when a chattering gibbon scared hell out of me as I had just dropped-off and I awoke growling from some place inside me I didn't know existed.

"Simple gestures. They render best," he said. "I'd say you spoke monkey that night. What's your story anyway? I'm grateful you patrol the hall at night but can't honestly see the need. Most residents is half dead and yearning for the blue light of the angel. And you ain't her, even in that gear."

By then I was leaning on the sink, holding the towel for Lucius as he trembled into his clothes. I could see the ache behind his eyes while he was doing his best to expose tender places in me. Like I was the shaky one.

There was a rapping on the door and a stern voice said, "Hey, somebody having a party in there? I gotta GO."

Lucius put his finger to his lips, said, "That's Hermione Heiss Hoffman, the one with the fat tabby. You know her feet ooze and she still goes around barefoot, leaves a trail like a slug. Wears that yellow sunflower muumuu that falls straight down from them orbs that's still firm as ostrich eggs. Don't worry. She'll move off to the facilities at the F'in' KC next door."

But she stayed in the hall a long time -- tapping, rapping, then yapping. This was her time we were displacing and she took it less graciously than Lucius did the cancer that consumed his cells, which he told me about as I dried him, and him withering down to soft bone mass like the world had reduced its offer of space above ground to its less active citizens. Which made me wish old Hermione a long line at the KFC.

I got Lucius back to his room, which is where he was determined to stay. He wouldn't let me call an ambulance. He wanted to tell me about the song.

"I wrote it for Johnny Cash, when my woman left me, of course, many years ago, and for good reason. I get mean when I drink and I was doing a lot of mean. I wore black Stetsons then. I swear, I was a great one for notions -- thought 9 to 5 at a meat packing factory weren't torture enough to make songs. Thought I had to divorce a good woman, knock-up a married one, outrun troopers on backroads, break nose cartilage in saloons. Hell, you name it! If it was bad for me or somebody else, I was for it. Still am. Say, junior, will you reach in the top drawer of that bureau and pass me anything solid you lay a hand on."

I had Lucius propped up in bed, and as he spoke I wandered like a tourist through his careless regard for privacy. Nothing was put away that I could tell, except the flask. He kept his door open so as I'd hump past his room on night maneuvers, I could see him chain smoking with a stack of 45's laboring the changer arm of a portable phonograph on his bed table that was always playing and always, like now, silent with the volume off. I had to ask.

"Oh, hell. I know all them songs by heart. Don't need to hear them to know they're there. Or maybe I'm testing the machinery. Or maybe I like the go-round motion. Or maybe it's the only thing left I got a license to operate. You need more damn reasons?"

"No! I get it," I said handing Lucius the flask. It was the only thing in there. Lucius said he liked his liquor in a cabinet ideally, like his Daddy, but that drawers were otherwise no worse than any other box to his thinking -- "cause there's no sense convincing yourself compartments hide secrets. They don't."

This was a homespun he lived by as I could see from the debris, a kind of archeology in layers from his stay here at the "degenero-rancho" (which is what my landlord called the place): a ukulele with one string hung on the wall along with a signed photo of Johnny Cash (fan club issue) and several rodeo ribbons from his son touring the Arizona shows. Then clothing -- mostly jeans and tee-shirts strewn everywhere. Lucius wore no underwear. Would probably slip off his body anyway. Coffee cups littered the table and bureau as did ashtrays. His one "dowdy habit" as he explained was collecting ashtrays -- one shaped like a deer, one the state of Texas, some from political campaigns and cigarette ads. All overstuffed nearly beyond recognition with ash and butts of ineffective lung protection. A Martin acoustic lay on a chair beside the bed.

As I was getting to know the man through his things and quirky homilies, warming up to him, the silver flask went smashing into the window, breaking glass and wedging into a diamond of chicken wire tacked from the outside that provided security from intruders. Then came two coffee cups, an ashtray with debris flying, and a cowboy boot.

"Shit, Lucius! What's wrong?"

"Nothing. Nothing. It's all right, in fact. I just want an open place to send my song. I want the celestial blue angels to know I'm coming. I don't have their welcome. I have wronged too many here on Earth. They want the ghost of Lucius Fenneman to linger and atone. But fuck them! It don't want to linger. And I don't want to atone. So help me out, boy. Kick out that damn wire mesh! Sing Halleluiah, son, and fuck-all to them angels!"

So I did. I did both. Then Lucius made me promise to agent his song. He said, "Consider this my audition," and he sang until that was all that was left of him.

Something Like A Buick

"I got dead eyes underside these Ray Bans, baby. I got this empty sleeve. What you think a little white girl got to do to sing the blues anyway? But we all *pays* for what we *gets*: stray dogs and back rent for me, married men and Jehovah's Witnesses, dry skin and a dry twat and no way to know if my teeth are clean."

She smiles.

"It takes a lot of wrong to get it right. Buy me one more of these."

Sunny raps an empty shot glass on the table. The Rolling Stone music critic, Caesar Schwartz, sketches notes, gestures a refill to the roustabout waitress.

"Ohhhh, box me up, baby. Wrap me in bows," Sunny whisper sings, sways in her seat, smiles, runs the one overbusy hand through her curls, pads with fingertips the table-top then picks a cigarette out from thick ash accumulating like compost in an upturned Cadillac hub cap -- car parts a decorator scheme in this south-end Chicago blues and funk revue.

"Why the clichés?" Caesar says. "Whiskey and cigarettes, the dangerous mouth?"

"It's a life choice, baby. No cliché to me. I like what leaves a mark, what scritches my voice and tears my flesh. I like to share what's cut me up. I'm a walking report card from the school of hard knocks. Save me Jesus! Save me Wall Street! Save me Rambo! Save me Jack Daniels! What's the diff? Ain't we all just Jelly Roll?"

"No jive, sister," Caesar says tittering. "I'm down with that," he says with cool. "But *your* filling could be different from most. That's why I'm here," the critic says smugly, puckering thin lips, peering into the Ray Bans, surprised by a wink. Do the blind wink? "What do you want Rolling Stone to do for you, Sunny?"

"Well, baby, since you ask, what I want is you should *NOT* do me the Ripley way."

"What's that?"

"That's put me in a see-through bottle, label me Little Miss-fortunate Blues."

"You'd rather be wrapped in a box."

"That's right, baby. Make it pretty."

"Look -- I wouldn't dis you. Your music moves me. That's why I'm here. You're a funk apotheosis. Just look around ... " Caesar's hand sweeps the room but flutters embarrassingly to the table. "Sorry, I forgot. But your sound is definitely not shaped for some curatorial setting. There's no pagan arias here. You stretch me back to patterns of the great verities: love, sex, loss, rhythmn. You shake me to the viscera. I can *feel* you. There's a volcano down there in your gut, mama's milk curdles down there, no amount of pink bismol is going to settle your dispute with the world. I like that about you."

"Oh, baby. You move me!"

"Really?"

"Not really, no. You don't know shit."

"You can't mean that?

"I mean, you lay the needle in the groove and go all soft and gooey like the band plays for you. It don't. It don't give a shit about you. I don't give a shit about nobody. When my guts get twisted enough, they unwind by their own self. They don't care who knows it. They don't let nobody *inside.* It don't matter who puts the quarter in the juke box, baby. It don't matter who puts the kettle on the heat. You can't feel my pain. But you sure can increase it."

"I wouldn't do that."

"Then wrap me in a box, baby. Tie me in bows."

"What are you saying?"

"Make me pretty."

"But you *are* pretty!"

"Convince me."

"All right. There's an old song. How does it go? Your teeth are sheep, your hair is goats, your lips are red… something, your breasts are deer, I think, your neck is the tower of David."

"Doesn't sound pretty."

"Yes, sorry. And not very original."

"That's right, baby. Nothing original about you. I bet you make love missionary. You got your six month dental marked on the calendar by the frig. You ride with the seatbelt hugging your tummy. You already got a retirement plan worked out with your accountant don't you."

"I'm afraid you're right."

"That's right, baby. You're afraid."

"But,"says Caesar, "you're wrong about one thing."

"What's that?"

"I absolutely do *not* ride with the seat belt on. I crank the radio and open all the windows. My tie flaps in the breeze."

"Ain't that a TV commercial?"

"How would you know? Oh, sorry."

"What do you drive?"

"It was my father's car,"says Caesar.

"Naturally. Not what I asked."

"It's a Buick, a sky blue Regal, 1976 with a 350 small block."

"That's right, and a 4 barrel carb, flair fenders on 15" rallys, buckets, tilt wheel, A/C and Hurst T-top, the Kojak car with schooner lines."

"Yes, I suppose so, but how do you know all this?"

"That's how I lost my arm, baby. The hydraulics that separates the frame and axle so I could squirrel up there and bolt down the leaf springs, it misfired. That car took my arm."

"What's that?"

"Can't you hear? I did chassis work for GM back in my Detroit motown days."

"You did motown?"

"No, I did GM. Some background with the Rayber Voices for Smokey Robinson, that's right, but only because them darky studio boys likes a little white chicken on their spool decks. But you won't hear much more than a squawk or two of me on tape. My best performance in that studio would not of been recorded. But, listen, how would you like to show me that car."

What's that?

"The car, *your* car. *There ain't noth-in' like a Bu-ick* (she jingles). That car. I'd like to touch that car again with the one hand it's left me."

The band has all this time been setting up on the platform, plugging-in and tuning-up. Sunny throws down a last finger of whiskey. Dooby Scott, her escort, the drummer with soft eyes, slides inside the booth beside Sunny, says, "Ain't she something, our Sunny? She's held up pretty good for all the miles, ain't she."

"Why, Dooby, that's no way to treat a lady. My miles is my own business."

"Ain't she something. Did you know Sunny had a thing with Bob Dylan?"

"That so? I'm no gossip columnist, Mr. Scott. But

if you think there are discernible influences. And, of course, Dylan's name does carry some weight in a paragraph of ink. This could be significant back-story, Sunny. What can you tell me about this?"

The band revs up on the stage -- a saxophone slips through scales on spittle-slick brass, a lead guitar does a wah-wah riff like angels moving through water, a harmonica goes fluttery with a dancing tongue, the Hammond organ huffs a bass note.

"Pure love fest, mister critic," says Dooby. "They was hooked up at the Montreal Jazz Festival."

"Really?" The note pad goes busy with scribbles.

"Yeah, that's right. I was there, Tonsils was there -- that's our harp player in case you forgot -- and Sunny was asked to do the dowap back-vocals for Jackson Browne. Much beneath her. But it was Dylan that took notice. That boy can read soul. Sunny was already hav-ing some trouble with her eyes back then, and the arm was gone of course, but that Dylan he knows where there's marrow to chew. Our girl, Sunny, she got some bone structure, don't she."

"Well, yes. I suppose I know what you mean."

"Oh, you *know*, mister critic. I seen your eyes wan-der her bones. I bet she feels the heat off them eyes of yours. She's very sensitive, you know, our Sunny. But like I say, Dylan, he dived straight to the heart of our song bird. He took her to his brass bed, he caged her in that brass bed, he ..."

"Dooby! please. Enough said."

"No, it ain't. I'd like to know who taught who about whatever. I mean, Dylan ain't done all them things he sings about. It's the rest of us have. It's Sunny that have. Hell, she must of toured all these 50 states from that broke-down station wagon of hers and has got the map etched into her hide to prove it."

"Why, thank you, Dooby. That has got a real complimentary sting to it. I do believe I might do a spread for TATTOO magazine off that recommendation. What you think?"

Dooby shakes his head in amusement -- tasseled curls jounce at the back of his neck, bald shines on top. He takes the cigarette from Sunny's hand and sinks it deep in a pile of ash. He grips the hand that Sunny dangles to help unwedge her from the vinyl bench seat of the booth and leads her to the stage, Sunny refusing to bump her way through space with the cane she holds. The wide planes of her face shine like Chinese lacquer in the hot lights, a cubist land-scape, all rectangles and triangles that slide and bend and refract light, not unflattering as assembled propor-tion: high floating cheeks and drilled dimples, a proud chin, pastry lips and a come-to-dinner breadth of forehead supporting a fall of blonde waves and thick brows riding the dark Ray Bans like butterfly wings. The glasses spark and glitter. The smile tenses, too perfect to be real so very real seeming as a conse-quence. A blood-red dress clings supple and fleshy, shimmers like water -- a nylon deep-neck, ankle-long,

long-sleeved, beer-stained Chanel knock-off sold in K-Mart with one empty-sleeve and undulations throughout. The whole of those parts that remain intact intimate and accessible to an audience because used and fearless of showing use and purposeful in all its motions.

When the music starts, Sunny closes her eyes from habit and caresses the microphone stand and sways as if falling into the soft, empty spaces between Hammond organ and saxophone licks. *"Watermelon man,"* she sings, *"bring a sweetness ripe and runny, make the fatness in my tummy, oh, do-bop-shabop, make the fatness in my tummy..."* Sunny runs her hand gently over the curve of her stomach, swings her hips, fills the interim with scat verse, surrenders to the musicians their moment then sings, *"Watermelon man, bring a sweetness ripe and runny, make the fatness in my tummy, have a care to stay till Sunday."* Her voice fades moanfully, lingering with a hang-note from off the saxophone.

Caesar Schwartz is on his feet whistling between fingers, turning heads, dangling the car keys like rhino horn. What is he thinking? Maybe that this is the most complete woman he's ever met? No, that's cliché. Maybe he wants the woman Bob Dylan had? Yes, maybe that. *Lay across MY big brass bed.* Or maybe he figures she won't be too choosy. Can't see, can't touch by half. His mealy face and crooked teeth and paunchy gut and fungusy feet, only the horse he rode in on after all, well besides the Buick, but it's his brain that's important, his writer's brain, and maybe what he can do for Sunny's career. No, certainly, she can't be too choosy.

Five, six, maybe eight more songs later. Caesar shivers with desire. She is *so* accessible, so very real. Women are just not like this. There hasn't been a scribble on his note pad since the last note of the first song. His skivvies have tightened uncomfortably. Her final song teases -- *Please, release me!*

Dooby helps Sunny off the platform, hoots of praise tremble on the greasy air, besotted patrons stick their eyes and hearts on Sunny's torso like tossing burdocks, glasses rap table tops, sloppy voices "God damning!" and "Shoot me, sister, now that I'm alive!" and "Hit me with your rhythm stick, baby girl!" Dooby Scott leads Sunny back to the music critic, kisses her cheek and fades toward the bar. The Rolling Stone man goes instantly gawky, advances hands to touch then pulls back, opens his mouth to speak but is distrustful of words, shuffles feet and finally crosses them, moves his eyes all around Sunny but finds no place to settle that hasn't been claimed. When tears collect behind the Ray Bans and slip away one diamond at a time down the side of Sunny's nose, he takes courage.

"Your music ... it hurts you. That first one especially, I think."

"Watermelon man."

"Yes, that one. Succulent, sensual, and the suggestion of seed, delivering on the backside, which is where funk resides. Really clever, very clever. And when you caressed your stomach, I have to believe there's personal history there."

"Oh yes indeedy. There's my daughter."

"Oh, I didn't know.

"First time I said so."

"Where is she?"

"Singing with the angels, I expect."

"Oh, I'm sorry. And the father."

"Watermelon man."

"Oh, yes, I see that now."

"He was a black man, a motown man, a voice I knew that took a shape I could touch, sexy from the roots of his nappy hair to the curl of his toe, and large in all his parts, especially his heart, which had a whole parcel of females in there I didn't know about right away. He shaped me like training a vine up a pole, he went inside me with his song and with his person, he gave what he could spare that weren't tied up in busi-ness and friends and wives and kids. He gave just enough to double me with life."

"He knocked you up."

"Yes, indeedy, up and sideways."

"Oh, that's terrible. Listen, Sunny, do you want to ride in the Buick? I'd be glad to give you a ride in the Buick. If you'd like."

"Yes, I'd like a ride in the Buick."

The night sky has October clouds bruised looking

but sharp as knives, moon lit, and velvety in-between with stars, lots of stars pulsing on a grid of high voltage, like making a play for daylight, like one day they'll make it. And the Buick, it flies down the road, windows open, radio tunes sucked into the night like most everything else in that car not bolted down, except for Caesar, who has got his seat belt pulled tight, and Sunny, who smiles thinly in the green tint of the instrument panel, runs her one good hand across the naugahyde, the dash, the quilted ceiling, the carpet floor, reaches behind to trace the chrome door latch with miniature ashtray, primo, perfecto, like straight off assembly, the scent of grease and rubber still potent and intoxicating. She runs her one good hand down Caesar's neck and circles his ear, caresses his thigh where the skivvies have stretched and strained, kisses and pets, sings *Box me, up, baby, wrap me in bows*, unlatches the seat belt and falls into his lap with those pastry lips, those perfect teeth and switches off the lights with her one good hand and presses down the accelerator with her one good hand, and they speed into the night, the critic closing his eyes, surrendering himself to the crush of metal and the tumbles and sparks all compact and altogether a perfect assemblage of car and flesh and dreams and song.

Pulling From The Bottom Of The Pile

When the train doors opened, Camilla stood in a press of winter coats waiting to assert themselves onto the platform and into the main hall of New York City's Grand Central Station. Another day of "the drabs" she thought, facing the backs of fellow passengers jostling the runway ahead in dappled charcoal, midnight black and the occasional tweed brown — mostly business garb, a kind of chastity wear to fender distractions of the flesh or of the spirit nature customarily plumes and tints. But even nature had given up. It had, so far, been a somber and snowless winter. From the interior of Connecticut, Camilla had begun her journey, a landscape of weed-choked fields anticipating the developer's blade. She had whistled down through small New England towns that lay trim but empty of purpose in the time between Christmas and Easter, then rattled alongside tenements boxy, sooty and graffiti stained at the edge of the city. She had found herself dream fuzzy the last few months: floating out-of-body like mystics or the clinically depressed, her senses thick as cotton, the earth less solid, flattened to a single dimension, rounded at the edges of delineation, bending in upon itself even as she traveled the vanishing point of the rail line. Camilla was curious about this new development, analytical, a little bit suspicious, but not ascribing to epiphany or breakdown.

When the man in the canary yellow slicker bumped her as she ascended the stairs, she sprawled in a bruised mass of flyaway papers and splayed limbs, his chummy apology and sartorial extravagance offending more than the physical battering. And there was plenty of that. Her knees were bruised and cut, her ankle badly turned. Manuscripts had slipped from the valise and drifted beneath indifferent feet. Recovery would be like pulling from the bottom of the pile.

The man in yellow fluttered above her. She could see beneath the wings of his coat a white safari suit with a yellow tie and an alligator belt all spinning on the points of cowboy boots cut from the same grouchy amphibian as the belt. His boots danced an arabesque as he retrieved papers from beneath Blucher Oxfords and Lexington wing tips. He told Camilla to "shelter here" at a bagel kiosk and bought her a coffee then led her deep into the terminal where a bench faced the quadrangle brass clock designating INFORMATION. He helped Camilla collate papers and offered medical advice: "torn and stressed anterior ligaments most likely, keep on the shoe, elevate, later apply ice." It seemed to Camilla that time advanced reluctantly, bullied out from its hiding place by a set of arms like tongs threatening from the clock above IN-FORMATION. She needed to compose herself, which she did best by discomfiting others, so began to critically assess this flamboyant jungle bird who had tipped her off balance: he was youthfully tan but middle-aged, sandy hair gone waxy gray but shag-cut and care-free tousled, the face open and friendly, eyes gray and clear, freckles riding wide cheek bones, your typical American boyish man, found lately fishing in the spring run-off of some remote river, and as a youth eternally trotting off the soccer field in a scrum of teammates and prankish laughter. A preppy face, a face like many a handsome poison ivy she had sparred with in her career -- publishers and literary agents, advertisers. His costume no more outrageous than a Tom Wolfe getup. While he turned her foot gently in his hands, she blinked at the vaulted ceiling where constellations dimly oscillated acknowledging the practical concern that New Yorkers will never see the stars otherwise.

"I know you," he said studying her face. She had drifted farther into Andromeda. Reluctantly Camilla fell back to Earth. A corona of staticky hair framed his overeager smile. Shoulders expectant of shared discovery loomed over her. He was no Tom Wolfe. There was something crass and pedestrian in his presentation, an exuberance of vestigial potency, like a flare-up of undervalued attributes before extinction. He was a dodo fanning tail feathers, strutting, emitting come-on vibes. She knew then why the dodo had vanished. It had no practical sense in choosing a mate. Camilla would never have crossed paths anywhere with this Ken doll mannequin festooned in Cabela and Banana Republic.

"I know you," he said. "You're Camilla Underwood. The beach party. I'm sure! You're her."

Shit! He was right. Only it wasn't soccer. It was football. It was high school. He was a half or a full or a quarter of some kind of back. One of the populars dating a cheerleader, of course, the brains and the nads (same difference probably) behind the Willow Lake winter weekend beach scene -- all those deserted summer A-frames with keys cleverly hidden beneath WELCOME mats, empty beaches, stocked liquor cabinets, a convergence of fat-tired Chevys and supercharged Dodges at midnight behind the A&P, convoy to the lake, the new party den already scoped out and then the break in and chugalug and drugs and sex in the bedrooms and busted stuff and getaway before the cops. These were the wildest parties, the best organized, the best known secret of Buckner High. By invite only -- every girl's dream to attend. Is this really what boys are about? she had wondered, uninvited, from the sidelines. She was a sophomore and bookish, but mature physically even if unsure what to do with it. "Cute" is what they said of her: all that dark curly hair and curious brown eyes beneath teased bangs and a cherry mouth and a wonder bread complexion. "Cute, very cute."

"I don't know you at all," is what she said.

A slap to the face might have had the same effect. His hands gestured awkwardly. His eyes searched for a neutral place to fasten a glance. He seemed anxious to move with the crowd that streamed out portals onto the sidewalks of 42nd Street and Park Avenue.

"You're not Camilla Underwood? I don't know you from high school?"

This was harder than she thought it would be. She needed his cooperation. Most would discern a simple brush-off and let it go, take a casual blow to the ego and carry it somewhere to bitch it out in private, or trot it out in the company of friends for a laugh, or maybe walk around with it for awhile as a bitter-sweet memory and excuse it. "Yes," she said, "all right then, I guess I am, or I *was* Camilla Underwood, but I am as-suredly *not* the same girl you took to that beach house. I simply wanted to make that point."

"Camilla, how could I think that? None of us are who we were in high school. Thank God for that, right? Look, I'll help you to a cab. I'm getting the mes-sage that Hot Rod Anderson isn't what you want right now. Stupid name isn't it. No one calls me Hot Rod anymore. Are you missing a meeting? Let me help you."

"No, thanks, Hot Rod. I'm fine." But she wasn't. She could not get to her feet without help, and her foot had swelled blue purple in here shoe while stretched out on the bench.

"Look, Camilla. You're in bad shape. If you're a commuter like me, and I think you are, you have an uncomfortable office waiting for you or an over-crowded emergency room. How's this for an alterna-tive -- I have a suite booked at the Beekman Tower just blocks away. I'm not hitting on you, Camilla. You can have the place alone all day to soak your foot, surf cable television, count the barges on the East River, whatever you want. Take the day off and heal, Camilla. I've requested a view of the United Nations so I can see the flags. I've loved those since a kid. I'm in town for a few days but taking meetings practically the whole time -- the loyal brotherhood of government contractors. My company builds bridges. I won't bother you at all, Camilla. If you can't trust me you'll never want to drive across another bridge, will you? Come on! How's that sound?"

How could it be that Camilla felt as though she were being maneuvered into another winter beach party? How could it be that Roderick "Hot Rod" An-derson could reduce her so quickly to the pubescent knot of insecurities that characterized her in high school. She had moved on from Hot Rod pretty quickly after the beach party, ignored boys altogether through the rest of high school, become valedictorian of her class, gone on to Vassar, president of her class, then to chief production editor at *Vogue* magazine --

sex surveys, starlet interviews, cosmetics advice, haute couture, dream destinations, advertising. If it's readable, it's Camillable. That's what her staff writers say. *I've been Camillaed!* the standard grievance. The meetings she runs are short, direct, and very, very unfriendly. Hot Rod was right: she had another such meeting scheduled for the morning. But lately her energies for trenchant observation, for accurate definition of purpose and surgical extraction of what lay beyond, were fading into vague tendencies of disinterest. And she had to admit, she knew Rod from the moment he knew her. And from that moment, she had released all she had become in response to what she had once been.

"I don't see how I can go to work today, not after this," she said.

"Then it's settled. I'll get us a cab and set you up in a nice room where you can clean up and heal. It's the least I can do for a classmate, for a friend I should say. Can I say friend, Camilla?"

"You can say that, Rod, yes. If it means enough to you, you can say that."

In the short cab ride to the Beekman Tower, Rod told her all the major events of his life after graduating high school: apprenticing with his father in the trades (custom kitchens their specialty), the cancer that had riddled his father's bones and taken his life, jobs shrinking with kitchen components redi-made, then Vietnam, then marriage, his wife pregnant again (three

kids end of count), and deciding to take a chance -- all
or nothing -- so buying piecemeal a fallen-down mid-
town block of Danbury near the old hat factory,
schmoozing town fathers for permits and tax breaks in
development. That's when he got to know government, how to open doors by paying attention to the
right people and judging response and riding the winds
of populist legislation. His townhouses were a great
success. Bus lines rerouted to collect his tenants, state
and federal money poured in. Everyone back in the
80's was looking for a fast solution to low income
housing in dying cities. Rod seemed to be the answer.
He got out before government money dried up, before
the economy faltered, and began to do the heavy work
of bridge construction. Again, perfect timing. Just as
Rod had shifted his operation, the news media were
sensitizing the public to concern for the nation's
highways. Of course it helped that that turnpike
bridge collapsed in Greenwich sending motorists sev-
enty feet into the Mianus River. Once again, money
poured in. Rod traveled the country to "re-bridge the
interstate." He monitored his kids' teen rebellions
from telephone lines and fathered on occasional holi-
days when the jobs were close enough to airports. The
marriage just kind of piddled away. Nothing dramatic.
Just nothing there after a few years on the road.

A man well-practiced in living between the stops,
Rod had timed his life's summary perfectly. The doorman at the Beekman Tower greeted the Yellow Cab as

Rod placed his hand on Camilla's knee and said, "I really don't remember much about that night at the beach house, Camilla. I'd like to though. I know I'm missing something." Rod smiled his school-boy radiance negating whatever Camilla might have understood as a come on.

Rod stepped out from the cab and whispered to the doorman, which made Camilla wonder how much of this had been planned in advance, another scoped-out job by the seriously inventive, happening Hot Rod Anderson. But no, it was to smooth the way for discreet aid for the injured -- a wheel chair appeared curbside in which Rod scooted Camilla beyond prying eyes through a service corridor and into the maids' elevator, bypassing the hotel lobby, and then the bell-hop keying the designated room which he opened with a flourish that telescoped the East River sending a wedge of sere light through the window upon which flags of many colors rippled across the street. Rod asked permission, disarming and sweet, and lifted her like a child from the chair and carried her to the sofa beside the window where he lay her down. He removed the yellow jacket and shone like aluminum standing in the sunlight in his white suite and polished teeth, beaming.

This was some suit: tailor-made in Mexico, Rod said, fitted to within ounces of body fat. The material is hemp, he said. Can you imagine *wearing* that stuff? It had a kind of raw silk look, and the severe taper suggested a tight body still. It's the suit O J was made to squeeze into during the trial that set him free, Rod said and laughed. He explained further the cowboy boots -- a gift from the Governor of Texas, shot in the bayous of Mexico and stitched on location. These were Rod's only business threads, he said. All else is more practical for supervising from pick-up trucks and crunching numbers on-site in office trailers, much of this time in the warm southwest it seemed, as Rod's golden tan had burned red and deep into the back of his neck. Rod walked behind the sofa, his face solemn and somewhat jowly with the weight of years as he pondered flags of the United Nations, said, "These will one day be all just one flag, you know. I have to believe that. I hope for that sincerely. I don't want my boys to go to war."

Camilla knew that Rod and some others of his scrum had signed with the Marines -- youthful swagger gone to lethal acrobatics in the jungles of the gook. But a father concerned that his children prosper in a safer, if duller, world than the 60's -- this was a new Roderick Anderson. Maybe he was right. Maybe Rod and she were now very different from high school. She had been surprised by how easily Rod had lifted her off the chair and into the hotel room. But she may as well have been construction material. She felt a bit more unsexy than she wanted to in the arms of Hot Rod Anderson. She couldn't imagine her husband ever lifting her like that. Dear Harlan Koskott.

Chamber of Commerce Koskott. The political con-science of small-town Connecticut, the man that walks to work and nods with sincere interest at his neigh-bors, the ballot counter at elections, the man born se-rious as taxes, whose work ethic rivals Sisyphus, the man who stayed at home with the kids whenever Camilla sneezed, the man who took a month off work for each of their newborns. Sweet Harlan. The man whose true mission in life was the priesthood but for that kiss in the choir of Saint Mary's Cathedral, and more kisses begged or stolen at Easter break from college, an eventual lip-sucking extravaganza in the back seat of Harlan's Plymouth Barracuda the follow-ing summer up until their cascading urges collectively urged Harlan to propose. And so he did, and so he became the indulgent father, the obsequious husband, the tepid lover.

Rod gathered ice from the wet-bar fridge and rolled cubes in a bath towel which he bent like a pipe-cleaner around Camilla's ankle. He handed her the TV controls and poured them each a Scotch. Do lunch in my name, he said (Camilla nearly crossed herself) and placed the room service menu on the floor beside her. He told Camilla to run a hot bath to relax in but keep the foot well out and upon a folded towel. He sent the front desk scavenging for crutches, bath oils and aspi-rin. The Scotch slid down his smile which he carried out the door all the way to his raucous, back-slapping session in government bilking.

When the door closed and Camilla was alone in the hotel suit, it became apparent, finally, how much emotion she had held back. Tears fell in a gathering flood and her breath thinned then panted then convulsed rippling out from her gut, her pulse sped, she balled her hands and struck her thighs and said, "You fuck, you fuck, you don't even know, you fuck!" She tossed the Scotch in one hand and the TV controls in the other at the nearest wall. The plastic casing burst open. Batteries rolled on the hard wood floor and gathered at the edge of a Persian rug. The glass shattered in a bloom of stain.

When Rod Anderson tapped her on the shoulder in the hallway of Buckner High School as she gathered books from her locker, she had said nothing, expecting him to apologize and amble off, or not apologize and still walk away. She thought he had mistaken the back of her head for someone else, and stared at him with wondering brown eyes and said nothing. Rod stammered, the one thing that made this seem real, and asked was she doing anything Saturday night? She was surprised that this was a difficult question for him -- Hot Rod Anderson, the one boy said to have slept with every cheerleader capable of doing the splits, and half the home economics class, the boozy waitress at the Picket Fence who flopped her glands in every young boy's face when presenting the bill, even the typing instructor said to be filling a need between husbands. Camilla never did answer, she was too unsure of her voice, but when he asked a second time, Camilla simply took Rod's hand out from his pants pocket and wrote her home phone number on it and closed her locker and walked unsteadily off to class. She never looked back. If she had, Camilla would have seen Rod jotting down her locker number beside the phone number on his hand.

The formal invitation came pinned to a pair of black silk underwear from Fredericks of Hollywood. The note said wear these the night of the date and RSVP by returning this note to Rod's locker, slipping it up under the vents (the same way the underwear got in Camilla's locker no doubt). Her first reaction was tittering nerves, then a spurt of anger at his counting her so easy, and then some curiosity as to how wild a party this will be. As an only child of a couple surprised late in life, Camilla had the unwavering trust of her parents, and she deserved it mostly. Her parents were lavish in their support of Camilla's interests -- her nervous, pimply friends traipsed unobstructed in and out the house anytime day or night, welcomed in various numbers at the evening meal; her collection of castaway pets had burgeoned into menagerie and were cared for and worried over by Mom who also deployed the family station wagon for weekend ballet lessons at the New Haven Youth Conservatory; her obsession for James Dean was financed by Dad, posters and biographies and fan club dues, escalating to stifled raptures late at night. Hot Rod Anderson was nothing like a James Dean. There was no dark, brooding intelligence, no pain of misunderstood youth. And yet there was danger, a worldliness of deed and a determination to matter as a significant "someone" in the world beyond small town Connecticut. Next day in school, she slipped the note back to Rod and waited to hear more.

Hot Rod's fire-red Firebird rumbled into the Underwood's driveway at eleven thirty the night of the party. There was no other contact by Rod before this. Camilla had given up thinking he was serious, but she knew Rod's car the minute its lights strobed her bedroom window after rounding the cul-de-sac of single-story bungalows. It rumbled, its muffler glass-packed, its timing off-kilter, stuttery in idle, all that power unsuited to hesitation, then Rod's voice schmoozing her parents who worried open the front door in their bedclothes (Camilla's friends never knocked). She could hear their surprised cooing and Rod's gracious *yes, Sir* and *no, Ma'am*. Camilla stepped into jeans, hesitated, then slipped out and into the underwear Rod had given her. She put the jeans back on, laced a pair of sneakers, hooked a bra then decided *what the hell* and removed the bra, squirmed into a yellow cotton sweater, a tight one. She replaced the sneakers with ballet slippers and ran to the front door telling her parents they would be back soon, just a late movie, grabbed Rod's hand and led him away just as he was explaining, "Yes, that's right; he rebuilds kitchens; has done a lot of work in this neighborhood." As they stepped into Rod's car, he said, "A movie? Hell I told them bowling." They had a long, tension relieving laugh after which Rod said, "Did you bring the underwear?"/"Sitting on them," said Camilla. They laughed again.

Camilla wasn't surprised the convoy waited for Rod in back of the A&P. This part she knew from rumors. Some of the kids were impatient so drinking beers already, taking push rides in gimpy-wheeled shopping carts left by the dumpster. But Rod's appearance sent everyone tossing empties and running for cars, a kind of Burt Reynolds *cannon ball run* of screeching tires and squealing girls. Camilla was thinking about what she had been missing up till now. Rod led the convoy and told her to crack him a beer and take one for herself, which she did, her first ever, and awful tasting -- like soapy water with fizz. But the effects were startling then sedating. She flopped in a stuffed chair facing the center of the party. Rod beelined for the liquor cabinet and mixed booze indiscriminately in a large bowl, a concoction he called "hammer brain," which the crowd absorbed. Someone found the radio and dialed in a New York City rock station, WNEZ, where the coolest late-night DJ of all time, Alice "the night bird," projected breathy whispers and played the latest in bootleg from the Floyd and Tull and Morrison. The party got cranked once Brad Sumner and Brittany Lynch notched up the turbulence with a lover's spat (the usual for them, and the ritual separation that started it all), which ended with Brad shoving Britt onto a sofa and jacking another dance partner -- Cheryl Pomeroy or "pompom," the girl with the exceptional bouncing chest. Tears and a moody withdrawal resulted in Jack Tierny, secret admirer, scooting alongside to comfort Brittany Lynch -- his arm squeezing her shoulder, his tongue probing deep kisses. Strip poker had several kids half clad in the kitchen; the dopers stepped outside onto the deck where they did the Cherokee knee bend in snow around a bong; the "scrum" were active with their fists, punching holes in dry wall and tossing empties into the lake; the corners of the family room got busy with make-out action, the more serious coupling going-down upstairs in the bedrooms. That's where Rod carried Camilla once she had passed out from several more beers and a cup or two of "hammer brain." He lay her down on a bed and covered her with his letter jacket, a kind of marking territory, or maybe a touch of chivalry. Rod went back to the party but returned once he had swallowed several more shots of "hammer-brain" and a few more sudsy beers, once nearly denuded from a run of bad luck in strip poker, and after tonsilling some girl in one of the corners of the room downstairs. But he didn't return alone. He brought two of his scrum mates with him:

"Let's see 'em."

"Yeah, take down them jeans. Show the goods, Rod."

So Rod removed his jacket, and the ballet slippers, then pulled down the jeans. There lay Camilla splayed on her back, arms over her head in that tight yellow sweater, all that curly hair flowing off the side of the bed, her cheeks flushed, mouth open, white thighs in black silk Fredericks lace, an adolescent boy's rape fantasy. The zippers came down as Rod backed out the door.

How can Rod not know? Camilla summarized from the hotel room. Once she had calmed her breathing, the foot began to throb. She took four aspirin and adjusted the ice pack. And yet, he seemed really to have no idea, even back then. Rod had met Camilla at her locker the next Monday, apologized for getting her so drunk, asked for another date which she refused and that was that. Rod settled back into his group of friends and Camilla back into hers. Even now, there seemed to be no remorse of conscience, no recognition that something horrible had happened to Camilla, that it was all his fault. He couldn't know. He couldn't possibly. No man could be so bold as to think he might thirty years later seduce a woman he has already raped.

After a nap on the sofa, after a nibble of smoked deli meats rolled in herbal cheeses spiked with toothpicks flying bright colors in cellophane, after an hour or two of a Noel Coward musical on PBS, Camilla crutched to the bathroom to pour a bath and soak in Castile oils. She napped again, briefly, in the tub and as she awoke, she found Rod standing obliquely in the doorway smiling at her. She smiled back. Couldn't help herself. He carried her again, this time without asking, out from the tub and onto the bed glistening wet. They made love sweetly, urgently. And after, she was surprised by his gentle attentions -- petting the inside of her arm with the backs of his fingers, combing wet curls of hair off her face, small kisses down her spine.

If this were Rod's warm down, she recognized the same as her husband Harlan's warm up. Maybe that's why she felt herself revved again and reached for Rod and this time made love to him so aggressively that the two of them rolled heavily off the bed onto the hard wood floor, she underneath, and banged into the night stand, the lamp tumbling and breaking into glass shards on the floor. They scratched and bit, rolled into each other like ferrets, slammed several times into the bed posts, struck the night stand, again, sending the phone down on top of Camilla. Her come-cry was as much a cry of pain as of release.

They lay on the floor salty and wide-eyed, laughing with embarrassment at such animal intensity. Camilla curled into herself to cover her nakedness once the passion had abated. He took her meaning and dragged the bed spread over them. There was tense quiet mostly, self-conscious laughter, some pulling glass fragments out from under the skin, some exploring bruised flesh. Camilla was the first to speak: "Listen, Rod," she said, "I know this is a bit awkward, but I really need to do this again." Rod was surprised, grateful, encouraged to read romance into what might have been a tumble for auld lang syne. Camilla asked if she left for work an hour or two early the next morning would Rod wait for her here in *their* room. He said he would cancel the whole day for her, fill the suite with roses, book a chamber ensemble, burn incense, hire an instructor in the Kama Sutra, anything she would like, anything at all. "Just a couple hours in the morning is all I want, really, just to finish this thing properly," said Camilla. So then, no burgeoning affair, no family break up, once maybe twice more in the sack and that's it -- so much the better, thought Rod. He gathered Camilla's clothes, wrapped her foot in an ace bandage he had bought at a drug store on his way back to the hotel. Camilla wanted to crutch away on her own and he knew well enough to let her.

When Camilla returned home, quite late, Harlan was beside himself with worry over Camilla's having missed her train and then the bruising (that which he could see) and the swollen ankle. Camilla told him how she had fallen on the stairs at Grand Central and spent the day in the Emergency Room at Flower and Fifth Avenue Hospital, the one uptown near the Guggenheim. She said she was exhausted and sore and needed to get into work early the next day to catch up on things. He understood. He always did. And he never pressed her for more information than she offered.

The next morning, Camilla left for the city two

hours ahead of rush hour. Harlan drove her to the train station and protested mildly Camilla's decision to return to work. No effect. Camilla had missed far too much, deadlines were gathering, writers getting away with sloppy posturing, advertisers waiting for the nod. The train ride into the city was happier and more sun-lit than she had remembered in recent months. The birds were gathering, colorful wings issuing song, enli-vening the fields; the small shops had transitioned overnight to spring merchandise. Camilla had chosen Geoffrey Beene -- a purple "car coat" of quilted silk tartar with gold thread, embellished further with black ostrich feathers; beneath that a pale-blue jump suit in wool jersey. She had unpinned and brushed out her hair. There were few passengers and the ones present smiled at the promise of daybreak. Even the tene-ments at the edge of the city twinkled at her, aphid eyed, sun reflecting off windows.

When the knock came on Rod's hotel door, he could not keep anticipation at bay. He really did feel that this might be the start of something, despite what Camilla had said. He and Camilla had shared more than sex, he felt, as he had never before been so can-did and confessional with a woman. This girl was a find, exciting and tender and smart. She was classier than his usual, but why not! He deserved the best. He had every right to be proud of what he had become. And he could use a woman that knew the city.

Rod was dressed in a white terrycloth robe, his hair

slicked back from the shower, freshly shaved, his smile uncontrollably aquiver as he opened the door for two of New York City's finest with hands at the waist where all that bad-guy restraint dangled from belts thick as I-beams and the largest of these (both were *big*) asking, "Roderick Anderson? Are you Roderick Anderson?"/The other saying, "That's him."/ Rod saying, "What? Yes, I'm Rod. What's wrong? Did something happen to Camilla?"/"Oh, I'd say something happened to Camilla, all right, Mr. Anderson. You are under arrest for the rape of Camilla Koskott."/ "Camilla Underwood?"/"Underwood? Is there another? It's this one here," the other said flashing a page of Rod's high school yearbook. "Did you have this woman in this room yesterday, Mr. Anderson?"/ "Yes, of course."/"Turn around, Mr. Anderson. You have the right…." The really big one placed handcuffs on Rod and pulled him backwards out from his hotel suite by the cuffs. "No, this is a mistake. We made love. There was no rape."/"Tell it to the judge. Where do you think Mrs. Koskott got all this?" the other said fanning like playing cards several evidential Polaroid's of Camilla's bruised face, her scratched and cut back, her swollen ankle. "No, that's not how it went down! We made love," said Rod. "This isn't high school. We made love. She wanted to. This is entrapment." /"Yeah," the really big one said, "that's what she said."

Love Fatigue

Henry was overdue for another mind-bending in shabby-town, one of those factory clusters of upstate New York, his hometown. Like that morning the argument ensued between him and lousy Rita meter maid. "But the damn thing's broken," Henry had said./"Honey, there's a lot of things broken in this town. Who you think is going to pay to fix it all up if not scofflaws such as you?" said Rita. But that wasn't the mind-bender. Not even close. It was surprising himself contemplating male buttocks jouncing in denim down the sidewalk, first notice on a reconfigured life. The "first coming" is what Henry had named this moment in a poem sometime later. These were hard-bodies shaking off night-shift dust, machine shop specialists, redi-fit and custom built, blinking in the light, itching out metal shavings that had sneaked in under their clothes, trucking on down to Joe Deitzer's Tavern and Pizzeria for breakfast beers and pickled eggs. A fellowship of men doing manly things. Henry had abandoned directly his manager's job at the supermarket and a barren marriage and pursued his evolving inclinations through the streets of Montreal. And after all that, he had landed in a cubicle office at IBM back in shabby-town.

Of all the cubicle windows of all the corporate flunkies that ever labored in the back offices, she had to walk into his parking lot view. Henry followed her progress traipsing the diagonal to a rusted Honda. The whole thing had started years ago with eye contact at a poetry reading for the literati at a local bookstore. She had glowed in the lamp-light at the lectern: her onion skin (the "invisible girl" is what she called herself, veins and blue-black organs floating visibly beneath), her red hair plaited in a Celtic knot, legs in black leotard, an embroidered peasant dress flouncing, bright red clogs. Then as his teacher, flirty innuendo in margin annotations on his poems which she returned days later than his classmates' work. Which had led to that drunken wet kiss at a reception for some blowzy Irish hooligan poet very full of himself, their kiss blooming in a coat closet scratchy with wool and edgy with giggles as her husband paced the hallway and worried the front door hinges calling her name. But it all dead-ended that day after class in her office cubby where Henry confessed infatuation with her and concurrent frisking with a young man of quality, a doctor in Montreal he had met when checked into Emergency after rough, nearly rupturing sex. The good doctor having had recommendations of position, which he had demonstrated soon thereafter. And at that moment, to see her again after so many years, when she waved at him, the blood went thick as sludge, the head went vertigo, limbs immovable.

Sarah had felt the short hairs on her neck go tingly, a familiar response to admiring eyes, attuned as she was to flattery, and turned toward the blue square building of stone and corrugated steel where a man's face hung suspended in a window. She assumed this to be her lover and waved. Sarah second-guessed, stood a moment braced against a chill spring wind that sliced the lot from off the frozen river. She reexamined the face and wondered whether she had made a mistake but waved again anyway and walked on. Mistakes were the hallmark of her relationships. She had been working calamitously toward a third marriage with a teaching colleague at the state college. He was doormat effusive and comfortably trust-funded, when an executive IBMer had come along in his BMer with the top down. Edward toured her through the Finger Lakes, his fingers making in-roads, and then through his wine cellar of upstate product lined shoulder-to-shoulder, martial proof of significant regional investment. Edward said he liked to give back. She had admired his pure, unaffected and ruthless lust for lucre and all that affords. She had come to his office to present three slim volumes of poetry that documented the last thirty years of her life. But she couldn't get past his secretary, the Jersey barrier, all that practiced nasal abrasiveness, a prepared face, red nails tapping. Sarah had to leave the poems with her, one whose stir in the waters of life was otherwise insignificant, just a ripple beyond the walls of that room.

Henry saw her again later that same day when the secretary was told to phone her on campus to apologize and to cajole a return trip to her lover's executive office. Henry saw her in that office, his own feeble labor of words trembling in his hand. Henry had worked his way up from the basement print shop to a windowed cubicle as editor of communications: i.e., the employee newsletter. She knew instantly that it was he who had looked down upon her from the window. She kept this to herself. Henry pretended not to know her, and from the embrace of an amorphous, tufted sofa studied the newsletter copy he would soon offer for approval, while she chatted the secretary in mock-friendship, buzz of the usurper, and glanced at him and called his name which hung in the air as a question for so long she said his name again. By the time Henry had emboldened himself, acknowledged the unavoidable intersection of past and present and prepared a response, she had slipped into the boss's office. Henry would have to wait.

Henry had always, it seems, had to wait. After the collapse of his marriage, an event as precipitous as a churning glacier, as dramatic as a balloon deflating in a closet, he had matriculated at the local state college and immersed himself in the books his learned friends had often alluded to, and he opened his arms to male strangers in the gaudy byways of Montreal's skin game. Henry was thirty years old then, a bit paunchy and certainly played-out in the heterosexual game, though handsome still, and willing, god knows, very willing. He began to evade daylight, truanting on Mondays to recover from weekends in Montreal -- suns and moons revolving outside hotel rooms littered with sex-party paraphernalia and he rising groggily victimized like alien abduction with medical probes. This was when Henry had met her, as a student certainly but hardly a college boy. He had brought with him into the classroom the anvil and hammer of city streets. He had hammered at the bulwark of civility with his poems. She had liked his adult neuroses, his eternally hung-over and bitter take on life, his homo-erotic honesty, his off-kilter self-assurance and abandonment of decorum. She too seemed at odds with her public life, independent of marriage, untethered, drifting on the edge of self-discovery.

Sarah flirted shamelessly in the IBMer's executive office, but as a kind of distancing. She sensed that getting in her pants meant nothing, but that as soon as he got inside her head, Edward would erase everything he could and scribble the walls with his grease pencil. Still, Edward seemed genuinely touched that she had presented him with her verse. He opened randomly to a page. He read: "The smooth distend of day increases with the length of you." He smiled, or leered. Either way it was not a pleasant face. She saw him run his imagination all round her torso like a slow dance. She felt violated and wondered if this were what she wanted: the punishing humiliation of the conquered. Why not just give it all up for a while -- the pretense of self-control, the clever phrase, the bashful peek under the covers at her soul in these thin volumes. Respectability? Who gives a shit anymore. Outside in reception sat a former student. He knows her, or at least that side of her the IBMer is straining to access.

Windows, framed spaces, boundaries, perspective -- Henry pondered these things while waiting to present his newsletter to the boss. What could Henry remember of his favorite Picasso (jeune fille in a mirror, or something): a woman sizes herself in a full-length mirror, one of those antique oblongs on hinges, and she seems to be pregnant and is rendered in blues and greens while the image reflected is red and spooky mystic and sexy and very much unpregnant. How can the self that his former English teacher projects, that person he knew during his college days, see anything more profound than fun-house distortion in his boss's eyes, those metallic orbs, those ball bearings that reflect only, that can't transform and release, that let nothing in to do so.

His own window had come as a reward for several gritty anonymous type-setting years of numb recovery from his dissolute immersion in drugs and sex. Henry had straightened out, though not *gone straight* exactly.

After his humanities degree from state college and
nowhere to go, the night shift in the basement of IBM
seemed a perfect way to earn a wage while leaving
room to poet on the side and to follow the boys into
Deitzer's Tavern and Pizzeria. If the Montreal weekends returned, well, who would notice? If the job got
pulled out from under, well, what's the loss? Then
came the workshops in desktop publishing, the tearing
down of old presses, and Henry well-positioned as a
writer and a printer to assume leadership of an operation taken down to one employee from three basement inksters, two of whom were released bearing
indelible blue-black stains. The original editor, a retired
professor, had resigned in protest, a limp gesture. They
were all hollow men before let go. Henry got moved
to days, placed before a window, and had the newsletter foisted on him like a second change in life.

Sarah had weathered well enough the vicissitudes
of a professional life in academe -- the petty jealousies
for turf, the chalk dust fall-out from these tiny explo-
sions; self-abandon intersecting the provocatively gen-
teel before the contraction and draining off of poisons
in ink; husbands that puzzled her in their minds like
reading a faulty blue-print; husbands that come with
children that whine like golem malcontents; her poetry
become more terse with the years, less enamored of
the world, more bitchy; and physically, what can she
say? Avoiding mirrors of late. Looking seriously now at
all those strategies of mid-life actresses who never age

-- the face lifts, the breast enhancements, the hair dye
and the sculpted wet look. Lately it was yoga from a
sense of duty rather than spiritual expansion, though
the waist expands nonetheless, the thighs gone spongy,
the hair more brittle and flyaway, the feet veiny and
nails tinting yellow. But the face and the eyes, the de-
meanor and smile -- all these still youthful and inviting.
Sarah knows the impression: she's a spirited filly, ebul-
lient, buoyant, tender and honest with a glow of the
intellectual prankster in her eyes. This is what's said of
her. This is not her.

When Sarah stepped out from her lover's office,
red hair graying fast and spread like a shawl, overlarge
silver and turquoise jewelry dangling, a hip-length low-
cut sweater of knobby wool flowing against her like
water, soft linen yoga pants very tight, and as Henry
looked into her eyes, his hands trembling, she said, "It
is you!" She took his hand in a practiced gadabout
party gesture, while Henry said nothing still and then
averted his eyes and frowned. She could feel the Jersey
barrier get fussy with the details of their liaison, fingers idling at the keyboard, tiny bat ears twitching. "I
would never have thought to find you here," she said.
"You and me both," he said sadly, which reminded her
of why she had liked this guy who had sat wasted and
sullen in the corner of her classroom by the window --
a man among babes and longing more than they for
the bell to ring and recess to begin. "Listen," she heard
herself say, "do you have time to catch up?"/"I have

this newsletter to proof with the boss."/"Yes, never mind. I forget. People that live outside the ivory tower punch clocks, don't they?"/"Yes. Tiny impotent violences. I'm off work at four, available at six," he said, having decided to challenge her effusions. /"Oh," she said gesturing surprise with her hands, feeling the secretary lean into her response. "Six it is then!"/ "Where?"/"I'll leave that up to you."/"2609 Oneida Street."/"Where?"/"My place." The secretary emitted a tiny moue of discovery. "Yes, that's fine. I'll bring the wine," she said and flowed out the door.

Henry winked at Cerberus, offered in his intimations the two cents worth required to ferry him across the threshold, and entered the boss's office at the heady convergence of hindsight and foresight, which if you don't know is a state of unfocus. Or maybe it was the vertical red and white stripes of the wallpaper, the starry-blue curtains framing the picture window in which the boss floated chief among the stars -- obscene impression of the American flag -- like you cut this guy and he bleeds greenback. The window double-glazed had been framed in weathered barn wood and tricked-out with bronze eagle curtain tiebacks repeated in a pair of eaglet statues top of a book shelf also cobbled from barn wood. The birds in mid-thunderbolt bore sashes with Latin mottoes which, if he could read Latin, maybe explained their grim postures. All lay beneath a fluorescent ceiling of wavy translucent plastic. Henry felt packaged inside a

Twinkie. The boss gestured come hither. Henry walked to the desk and toward the view out the window of a landscaped, woodsy dell of trimmed evergreens and recycled water descending a cement stairs, bumping over colorful stones angled to a mesh drain, the sum of all enclosed in a stockade fence beyond which lay, barely discernible, the parking lot his own window gloried in.

"Listen," said the boss, "the newsletter can wait. In fact, I'm sure it's fine." The boss lay the proofs on his desk and crabbed backward on casters, arms bracing the back of his head, wingtips crossed on the ink mat. "I have a personal matter of concern, if you don't mind." The boss waited a brief, polite moment, having discounted protest. "Listen. It's this." The boss shifted his feet to the floor, rolled belly-up to the desk, placed his elbows on the ink mat, twined his fingers. "It's this thing I hear about your personal ..." The boss said, "It's this thing I hear ..."/"Homo shit?"/"Oh, well..."/ "That's a long time ago. It's in my past. I had a busted marriage, a very unsatisfying love life, a very cold wife. Stuff like that. So I broke gender. You ever imagine doing weird shit like that?"/"Well, no. I don't. Not like that."/"Okay. You got me. I'm queer. But I put together one hell of a newsletter, and I make no fuss. If anything, I've gone a-sexual over the years. The mailroom cuties have got nothing to worry about from me."/"Well that's great, really. I'm pleased. But what I wanted was to discuss a mutual friend of ours."/"Oh, you mean ..."/"I know you were once a student of hers, and I would very much like to understand these poems." The boss drew out from his desk the three slim volumes. "I know this is a bit off-task," he said, "but I need from you a line-by-line analysis of a couple or three of these poems."/"Which poems?"/"I don't know. You choose. Just tell me what they mean and they're instantly my favorites. Do you see?"/"Oh ... yes."/"Good! Listen, drop everything else for a day or two. Hell, take the rest of the week off ... no, make that the rest of the day. Just bring me those poems in the morning and I'll be in your debt."/"No debt necessary. This is a very small thing."/"*NOT* to me! You have me by the balls! Oh, no offense."/"Where's the offense?"

Walking the hall between cubicles on the worn gray carpet with fluorescence buzzing overhead, Henry imagined squeezing those balls. "Squeal like a pig!" he would say to his boss bent over a tree stump with his naked bum in the air, Henry hovering with an engorged prick in his hand. "Deliver me," his boss would say. Henry knew this wasn't a very mature response to the kind of professional relationship building he might use to advance ... to advance where? Henry turned into his own tight little office, walked to the window and realized where -- the next best view of the parking lot! An office of his own gussied in colonial decals! What had happened to him over the years? Had he gone from dissolute to diluted? What had become of his imagination? He couldn't imagine. He seemed to have made the choice to abandon an infinite wanderland in favor of property debt and mind-numbing cubicle certainties, the length and breadth of diminished possibilities.

It took meditating through a stretch of the usual road -- gliding past the boarded windows of downtown, wending through asphalt repair, idling at a R x R signal barrier (its red lights and bell pulsing him to near spastic), a SantaFe Warbonnet diesel coupling and decoupling up and down the line -- before *he* could enthuse over a visit from a poetess titillater, some ten years in arrears, now hot for his boss. His father had liked to take the family to the Round House down at the river bridge to watch engine repair. It was the one masculine thing Henry had enjoyed with his father, and it ended when Henry came out of the closet. He had to, Henry had said to his father, because he had married Imelda Marcos: there was no room for him; *taming of the shoe* best describes his marriage, Henry had said. Certainly, his wife was a bitch. His father had probably died from the shock of his confession. Henry wondered whose confession would end his own life.

Once at the strip mall, Henry made the rounds of a supermarket deli (pigs in a blanket tickled his wickedness; he chose instead brie cheese and matzo) and a package store (Scotch whiskey appealed; he chose instead an Australian chardonnay). Henry saw his life story in the third-person, omniscience omitted, denouement already concluded. He thought her life would be as easy to read. Yet when he sat down in his den and opened the first volume of her poems, the lyricism surprised him. She looks for completion, and from a host of things: items leftover from broken marriages that inhabit a place in space but not in her heart; exotic and complex settings that regard her as a tourist no matter the price of admission; silent and deep wounds that separate the brain from the viscera making her calculating one day and sympathetic the next; tiny organisms of regret that feed off the host they eventually destroy. Would Henry tell his boss about all this? Expose the umbra of her soul to the boss's insensitivity? Henry had never read her poems before this. How come? Probably too self-absorbed back in the day. What he had taken for her exuberant self-assertion had been, had always been, a kind of leaning after the sun of a house plant tucked in a dark place.

She walked into his house at precisely 6 p.m., in step with her infernal, internal clock watching, a pho-bia bred of her having been reared by stage parents, a life of timed exits and entrances that went off-kilter when a lorry strayed from its lane on the M20 outside Dorset, England, closing the curtain forever on a trav-eling production of *Faustus*, and she packed-off with Aunty, also an actress, to descend on America in a rush of wardrobe boxes and news clippings and time tables, following the seasonal trade of dinner theater up and down the East Coast. As a teen she had dropped off the truck and rolled away ("my little cabbage," Aunty had called her -- names are destiny). She had shacked up with a bald-headed waiter with a yellow goatee who sold his novel and left for New York City. From that moment she had begun to create a world for herself in poetry.

She was sure his house plants were smiling at her, luxuriating in their tropical setting on the thermostat, shiny hibiscus, spider, banana, Norfolk pine, Christmas cactus and geranium dripping spritz pools of water onto wood floors. And nothing meticulous throughout (there goes the stereotype): books piled on tables and chairs (her own poems wing-spread over an arm rest), ties draped, a crane-necked floor lamp, dishes with food remains littered the floor beside a favorite chair, the TV loud and snowy with poor reception (Dan Rather functioning as radio) while Henry called from the kitchen for her to kick aside the debris and make herself to home. Except for the books, there was nothing here to indicate a radical intellect, nor cathartic orgies, nor an artistic sensibility. Who was this man she had been so attracted to ten years ago? All the windows had double interior shutters opened at the bottom for plants and latched at the top for ... for what? She squatted to peek out and saw another small cape like his, chunky and cute just twenty feet away. She toured the windows of the den to see identical views from all directions. "Have you noticed?" Henry said, bringing a tray of crackers and cheese. "The view? I'm living in a cube. Same view all around.

Sometimes I get dizzy looking out that view, like I've been spinning around in here and landing at the same window each time."/"Oh, I hadn't noticed. The plants like it here!"/"Yes, they haven't complained."/"Do they talk to you?" she said to lift the mood./"Not in the normal way, no. But they do talk, yes."/"What do they say?"/"They say, say something real."

She reminded herself that this is why she used to like this guy -- his dreamy imagination, his penchant to cut through the bullshit, offenses falling where they may. She smiled at him and took a cracker off the plate, smoothed a glob of Brie over the baked surface and stared at him until he lowered himself onto the edge of a chair, the plate in one hand the other combing his thinning hair. Henry coughed uncomfortably. "You have my poems," she said./"I'm supposed to fathom their mystery," he said. "I'm not feeling right about this, because, as I'm sure you know, it's my boss wants me to figure you out."/"Yes," she said. "I understand. I'm homework."/"But what makes me feel worse is that I realize it's me wants to know. I'm treading unresolved waters here."/"Me too. Up a creek named shit."/"Yeah, that's the creek."

They laughed then became embarrassed. They avoided looking at each other. She put the cracker in her mouth and bit down. Her smiled wobbled. He began to shake with emotion. He stood up and flicked the cracker tray at the wall like a frisbee, food exploding in clusters. He laughed like a bedlamite as she choked on her own response then lung-launched a half-masticated cracker into an already polluted corner of the room. "Poets!" he said. "God damn poets!" And they laughed some more.

"We could sleep together," Henry said, then lowered his eyes. "Yes, she said, "I had thought about that, but I'm not the same woman you were attracted to ten years ago."/ How's that?/"Well, my flesh sags. My breath is off-putting. It takes a jack hammer to bring me to orgasm. How do you feel about the idea?"/ "A little more uncertain than I was a minute ago."

She reached for his hand.

The next day at work, Henry avoided the boss and Sarah avoided the phone. When he answered the phone, the Jersey harpy, nostrils dilating, demanded he stop in at the office straight away.

The Dean of Faculty invaded her office to verify rumors of a very public liaison with a rather garish IBM exec while her intended defended her hopefully, hopelessly, shamefully. How can she be so cruel? Reflects badly on her professional integrity, consider tenure pending, and so on.

He found his boss eager for his report on the poems and quick to assign industrial sabotage to his lack of readiness. Henry can't be interested in this girl? He's not into women, right? Why so stingy with her secrets? This kind of uncooperative, irresponsible behavior could jeopardize job security, and so on.

She said to the Dean, "What the hell business is it

of yours?"

He said to his boss, "You give me every reason to swear off men."

They met again, coincidentally, shortly after, in the parking lot at IBM. There was just one question on each of their minds: whom had she come for? Henry standing in one marked lane and she in another, they turned their heads toward the serrated tips of a stockade fence where a pin-striped man inside the building was breathing hard onto his view from a picture window framed in starry-blue curtains, fogging the window with agitated, empty speech, tiny pink hands greasing the dewy obstruction and then balled into fists pounding the thick double-panes. When Henry stepped over the line, they closed their eyes and embraced in a dizzy limbo of canceled regret.

Broken

Things were getting tense up on University Hill. Nested among the mercantile uppity-ups and Brahmans and the academic honchos, the Reg and Gladys Needham domicile was wracked by bickering, especially after Gladys had embarrassed them both at a faculty party (but embarrassed Reg especially). Madame college president pinned to an oriental rug in red heels blathered courtly and numinous beneath a glass chandelier -- Ruth Van Patten, cool as paint in her royal blue suit with the ruffle of pink spilling out from a suggestion of décolletage at an intersection of double-breasted lapels, holding a blush of Côte du Ventoux by the stem. And there foundered Gladys, a cow gone loose in the garden in her gauzy summer number of embroidered roses twining like poison ivy a high bodice cinched with a red ribbon -- a Bronte throwback that belled-out in a loose fit of the slightest suggestion of pleats. Of course Gladys didn't expect many to get the literary significance, or the personal significance. No one there, she figured, read much beyond the first five chapters of anything outside (or inside, for that matter) the *Readers' Digest* top ten beach list. If anyone asked, she was Jane Eyre to Reg's Mr. Rochester, having finally admitted to herself that he keeps another wife, one gone mad, up in the attic. Her auburn hair slipped lopsided in a bun stuck through with quills of Japanese lacquered pins that often dislodged and fell to the parquet with Gladys kvetching, rueful, picking them off the floor and sliding them back in and picking them off the floor again, carrying an emptied bottle of gin by the neck like trophy kill.

"So, Gladys, or Doctor Gladys of the Doctors Needham I should say, and that's a lovely dress,"Ruth Van Patten gushed, "I am most earnest in wondering what we may expect by way of published scholarship from you, my dear? I am sure you are working on something ground-breaking. Dean Lussac tells me you are one of his brightest and most promising."

"Nice of him. Thank you, Doctor Van Patten. But I have surrendered my position as tribal griot, yes, no more tom-toms in the night, no more dreaming over desert pouches, callipygian fantasies as we say in the field. I'm working up a fanzine on theories of conjugal homicide just now."

"How is that?"

"Well, shit, Doctor, you've been married and divorced and married and divorced haven't you. What good academic hasn't? Maybe you can tell me -- what's new in that since the lusty Wife of Bath changed her men like worn-out panties? Did you kill any of yours? Did you know that in the middle ages a nail tapped in the cranium worked excellent well, yes indeedy -- tap, tap, tap, just under the hair while he's sleeping. No blood. No muss. Hell, no husband! Ever try that one -- huh?"

"Well, no, Gladys, I have not. Reg!" Ruth Van Patten gestured above the nodding press of gray hairs with her free arm straight as a post and an index finger beckoning.

Reginald knew that tone of voice, the implied contretemps, and blanched when he saw Gladys tipping on her heels in a belly laugh of daring-do.

"Dr. Van Patten, how are you? Is Gladys showing off her aerobic jitters again? She is more animated than a scarab beetle in a tungsten lamp, I swear," said Reginald with his hand stretched out for shaking several feet before he reached Van Patten, oozing sang-froid.

"Keep a civil tongue, you damned, you... well!" said Gladys. "That's exactly how I feel around you these days, Reginald, a June bug in January. Ha! Did you think of *that* metaphor man? Did you? Do you even know what damn season it is?"

Gladys lifted the empty bottle to her empty glass.

"Oh, crumb! Time for a refill." And she tilted off into the buttoned-down tweeds and Herrington wools of her colleagues in her loose weave of summer cotton. When she found herself manhandled out the door by Reginald who repeated the phrase "Provost, my God, Gladys, Provost, Provost!" like a mantra with his sour breath fogging her glasses, Gladys knew she had gone too far. She didn't care.

And she didn't care all the way home in the car. Reginald moved tenderly through the gears of his classic '62 Jeep Wagoneer with the faux oak siding that he polishes weekly in the garage with fine steel wool and tooth paste because it's metal not wood and Reg wants no rust. Gladys lay her feet on the top of the dashboard -- "to warm them up in the defrost, husband" -- is what she'd say if Reg complained, but he knew enough not to complain more than necessary tonight. Keep focused on the one essential problem and meaningful correction may result. God, she is such a child.

Gladys bowed her legs so the dress slid past her thighs, as if to say, sure you can look, you bastard, but you're not getting any tonight. She poked at the buttons on the radio, then dial-tuned her way through schlock and commercials, bypassing all the pre-set favorites, just to drive Reg crazy. He tried not to notice. Reg drove through the lanes past lamp-lit, painted-lady Victorian homes that Gladys had dreamed of owning when she had first started dating Reg, or screwing him in the office would perhaps be the more accurate description of their early courtship. Who knows who Reg is screwing in the office now: all right, leave the brain outside the door and bring that twat to Daddy! Gladys couldn't for the life of her imagine how she could have fallen for the advances of this pusillanimous, self-serving and inflated Mr. Rogers cardigan man with the persistent residue of blackboard chalk. What did she see in him?

"Listen, Gladys, I don't mean to be a munch, but this public acting-out has got to stop if you want us to get ahead in this university. I mean, Provost for God sake! We may never get another chance."

"We, *we*? What is this, the *royal we*? What the hell *WE* are you talking about? There hasn't been a *we* in this relationship since I let down my panties."

"That's crude, Gladys."

"Yeah, big boy. The truth can be a little raw some-times. Would you like another dose, or are you already too weirded out?"

"What do you mean?"

"I've been thinking of ways to kill you."

"What did you say?"

Just as Gladys mentioned conjugal homicide for the second time that night, Reg had pulled into the long drive of *his* Victorian lady, the one he purchased during his first marriage as tenure had become as-sured, and drove around the carriage porch then straightened the vehicle in the direction of the garage and hit the electric eye over the top of the sun visor to open the door -- all a matter of routine timing. The slightest pressure on the brake to save the rotors, a gentle motion arrest that's easy on the springs and in this snow a worthy method of avoiding skid, since Reginald seldom uses the four-wheel-drive as transmissions are awfully expensive to fix. And the car would likely never come back the same. But when Gladys said "kill" Reg had uncharacteristically hit the brake which threw off the timing as the tires had gripped gravel beneath the snow and altered the effects of Gladys' usual exit from the car -- swinging the door open and stepping out almost before the car has stopped inside the garage, as was her habit. In this case, Gladys' door swung open, her leg went out, the door hit the frame of the garage before entering same and bounced back onto her leg as the car entered the garage. Gladys did not scream. Her leg went numb. Her shoe filled with blood instantly. The tibia and fibula had both cracked and punctured the skin as Gladys' leg swung straight down like a doll with joints twisted out of place by a bully.

"Holy shit. Holy shit. My leg. You've broke my fucking leg, Reg," Gladys said in a near whisper before passing out.

After the operation and pin-installations, Reg spent a month nursing Gladys back to ambulatory once she was released from the hospital: dashing home between classes (if, indeed, Reg can be said to "dash") with carry-out from The Bronze Gong, her favorite restaurant; back rubs in the morning with cotton gloves because Gladys complained of his cold hands, and sponge bathes in the evening with Glady's periodically succumbing to tickle spells; Reg reading her mail to her with a curious awakening to the large number of friends she has; and Reg condensing and interpreting the lead stories from two out-of-town newspapers and the one local; bringing the latest campus gossip to her evening meal including his closing on the Provost position and any sniping done on that count from jealous colleagues with appropriately mimicked accents and gestures (making Gladys guess the offenders); Reg speaking repentant gracious words to her mother who called regularly to assess Gladys' progress and the damage done to the marriage. She had been waiting for years for Gladys to fall back into the cradle from which she had been snatched.

But Gladys was having good sex now that Reg seemed genuinely solicitous, concerned for her well-being, and maybe some of his own, as having Gladys off campus during this particularly tricky political maneuvering toward that Provost job made the ascendancy almost assured, a kind of primogeniture of the most deserving. And what about that libido! Reg took Gladys with the pneumatic hammering of a man twice his youth, propping her up in chairs, setting her spread upon the vanity, wedged into the hallway stairs, even once in the car on the way to a doctor visit, before they had left the garage. Gladys was getting the best sex of her life, and she knew it -- opening her arms to him each time he appeared in her bedroom. But this also worked to remind Reg that he had neglected his professorial mentoring of late. So many nubile admirers and so little time left to enjoy their attentions. Reg started banging college chicks again in the office. He was on a roll.

Gladys answered the phone -- so many calls to Reginald for office visits, so many girls, ALL girls. Gladys knew what was going on. She began to indulge further in her studies of "illuminating homicide," as she called it, in particular the strange tale of murderers Burke and Hale that she came to in a translation of Jorge Luis Borges. Gladys began to work the case around in her mind. Lord knows she had plenty of time to think.

Those two Irishmen had gone on a killing spree in 19th century Edinburgh. They had lured victims from the streets to a garret lodging, gave them whiskey to drink and asked to hear the most unusual incidents of their lives. Once a victim approached the culmination of his life story, Hale would close his hands over the mouth from behind the settee while Burke would sit on his chest watching the last escape of living breath and look into the eyes for the unspoken final thoughts of the dying. It was a reverse Scheherazade, as the Frenchman Schwob has said, where the killer becomes indifferent to the end of the story, having decided that all of even the best tales of human suffering and accident and triumph are endlessly similar. Burke ultimately convinces Hale to take their murdering to the streets, where they cover their victims' mouths with rags soaked in pitch and dispatch them quickly -- minimalist artists in their reductions. Fascinating!

thought Gladys.

And then, of course, the phone rang. Gladys picked up and snorted, "When is it you want to meet Doctor Needham to fuck, honey. He's got a full schedule today. Could I pencil-dick you in for menstruation Tuesday? He's needing a lot of lubrication these days."

"What? Has Reg got a pimp service now? I'm Donna Massinger. Well, I am now. I was once Mrs. Needham. Is this Gladys?"

"Oh, shit, fuck, yes, sorry, sorry, sorry, the wife in the attic. Shit! It's me, Donna. Gladys that is. It was a joke, really. I'm sorry. Reg and I play these games, you know."

"Yes, I know about Reg's *games*, Gladys."

"Okay, look. I guess we're compadres in a sad kind of way. Things aren't going too well right now between me and Reg."

"I warned you, Gladys. I tried to. Anyway, I'm out of his range, finally. Things are going well. In fact, I'm thinking of remarrying. That's why I called."

"Oh, well congratulations! And, well, good luck, I mean, not that you'll need it. I mean not this time."

"Look, I'm not calling to invite you to the wedding. I want Reg to give me an annulment. It's important to my fiancé."

"Oh, right. Got it. Sure. I'll see what I can do. I mean, I'll pass this along to Reg."

"If you should finally deliver *one* of my messages

to Reg, this would be the one most devastating to him. Tell Reg I'll call in a day or two. I *was* thinking about calling his office, but I know what goes on there. Good luck with that asshole."

"Yeah, thanks. I'm thinking about killing him."

The line went silent, no response from Donna. Gladys said, "Donna?" Then she heard a click and a dial tone. What a bitch! Gladys had know she was a bitch from before she became interested in Reginald. Donna's bitchiness had made the affair palatable. And when she caught onto them, banged on the office door with her shoe until half the science department had leached out into the hallway with their petri dishes in hand and protective goggles strapped to their foreheads, no one could blame Reginald for doing what he had to do to escape this banshee from the Bronx who never did fit in around there anyway. And when Gladys had taken over as matron of the house on University Hill, she made wholesale changes to wash Donna out of their lives: a complete new wallpaper and paint job in lemons to remove Donna's brooding mauves and pale lavenders; out with the maroon curtain brocades with their gold tassel sashes and replaced by white lace with a flitting hummingbird pattern; many artsy vases fell to untimely demise as Gladys dusted clumsily ("oh, darling, sorry, another accident today"); the painting above the mantle of the Chateau Frontenac of Quebec City where Reg and Donna had honeymooned that Gladys replaced with a Kantoo tribal mask carved of a baobab tree that was supposed to ward off evil spirits (something she never told Reg); and finally, all those phone messages Donna had left with Gladys during the first two years of their marriage that she had failed to deliver. I mean, that woman was unbalanced, wigged-out, an uptight P.M.S. floozy going through emotional meltdown. Gladys couldn't entirely get her out of the house, no matter what she did.

But lately, as she felt her wounded body conform to the mattress depression that had to have been made by Donna, and as the phone calls from coeds to Reg increased, and as she thought about the wrong done herself and Donna too by this selfish man, Gladys decided to place Donna back in the house and then disappear quietly from Reg's life, leaving him to wonder if, indeed, he really had been married a second time.

Gladys began replacing the artsy vases she had broken in the early days of her marriage, pieces ordered through catalogues that looked about the same or that had the "feel" of Donna. Reg didn't notice. But when the interior decorator left Gladys' bedside with a sizable contract for restoring the woodwork and walls and curtains to maroons and purples, when the crew showed up with their steam-heat wall-paper peelers and fresh paint, and when the new curtains went up shedding a blood-red glow of gloom upon the dining table where Reg takes his coffee in the morning, he noticed.

"Jesus, what the heck is going on, Gladys?"

"I was thinking we could both use a change, Reg."

"But this isn't exactly change, is it Gladys? I mean, it all looks vaguely familiar, you know. It's pretty close to what Donna did with the house. Don't you think?"

"Oh, I hadn't really noticed, Reg. Indulge me, will you, honey. I just need a diversion, and you're always so busy at work."

That shut him up, but when she replaced the African tribal mask over the mantle with a new print of Quebec City ordered from their chamber of commerce, Reg had had enough.

"What are you doing, Gladys? It took me forever to get that woman out of my life and now you seem to be inviting her back in. Why? What's going on?"

"Reg, if you must know, I am making a statement here."

"Whatever can that be, darling? You know I don't love Donna. It's been you all these years."

"Yes, that's true, Reg. I'm sure that's true, so long as we don't count the others."

"What others, Gladys? There are no *others*."

"No? Well, hand me that note pad by the phone, will you, darling? Yes, thanks. No, don't read it. Just give it to me. Good boy. Yes, here then: Effy called to say she might be a few minutes late for her office visit. I told her you'd probably start without her. She's a cute number, Reg. I can tell. But there's a slight lisp. I won-

der if her overbite might make the blow job a bit difficult. Does it, darling? Let's see. Oh, yes. And here's
Joanna who at least had the manners to be nervous
with me over the phone. Bless her! Imagine a conscience in one so young. Could she have been a virgin,
Reginald? Ah, yes, I thought so. Isn't that just wonderful. Picking cherries at your age. I'm impressed. And
now here's ...."

"All right, fine. I can see where you're going with
this. You know, Gladys, and I hesitate to bring this up,
but you're no saint either, Gladys. You know you're no
saint. I've seen you in the kitchen with our male dinner
guests. I've seen your hands caress the shoulders of
strange men. Awfully suggestive if you ask me. In fact,
it ever you should want to carry this peccadillo of
yours into the courts of law, I'd say we have offended
equally. Well, yes, making appropriate adjustments for
what's thought appropriate for women. And you know.
I'm sure you know. In a court of law, women blemish
very easily, yes, very easily indeed. There will be no
fleecing Reginald Needham, my dear. Don't you even
think of that."

That's when the food hit the wall and some parts
of Reginald, the carry-out Thai noodles and kaffir lime
and prawns and chopped cilantro, and then Gladys
ordered Reg out of the house.

"No, Gladys. That's impossible. This is *MY* house
after all. I mean, surely you see that. Let's just calm
down."

"I don't want to calm down, Reg. I like this anger. It's purifying. Oh, yes, I think so. I want to do some damage. What do you say to my setting fire to this damn place if you're not out of here in ten minutes."

"You can't be serious."

Gladys leaned across the bed and set fire to the bedroom curtains with a BIC lighter she kept by the bedside for her periods of sleepless meditation with a joint but in this case trimmed to exude a torch-like flame. Reg swanned across the bed to rip down the curtains but landed on Glady's injured leg. She shrieked with pain and surprise. The curtains disintegrated before Reg could get near them but did no more damage than blacken the ceiling and send a fairy dust of carbonaceous threads adrift in the air.

"Oh, Gladys, how could you! These are radioactive isotopes you've released. We're breathing poisons!"

"Come on, Reg," said Gladys pushing him off her leg. "This is harmless soot. Be a man, will you?"

"Sure, sure, what you don't know won't kill you. That's what you're saying, isn't it? Tell that to the women that died of phossy jaw. Did you know they licked the tips of brushes and painted the dials of clocks with radioactive phosphorescence? Did you know that? A slow and painful death. Believe me."

"Preach me no lectures, Reginald."

"I'll not stay here and breath myself into the medical books. I prefer to die of natural causes."

"Good, because if you don't get out of this house

soon, there will certainly be nothing natural about your death. Get out! Out!"

Reginald knew enough to avoid a scene with Gladys once she had become so raw. He knew her strength in that regard. So he threw important papers into his briefcase and an assortment of cardboard boxes, pulled out and stacked the dresser drawers that held his clean underwear and socks, rolled up and tossed his trousers and dress shirts and sport jackets into plastic garbage bags and set out for the Uptown Hotel for what he figured would be a brief stay. Gladys saw the blinking red tail lights of the Wagoneer drift out the drive and nearly leaped out of bed to celebrate! The cast held her back, as did the pain. But the exuberance nearly overwhelmed her. Gladys had bested the big bad sophisticate. And she had done it with style. Damn she was good!

Several days later, Gladys had thought about and ruled out the following: a high profile divorce implicating all of Reginald's "little darlings"; burning down the place in the hopes that the fire would spread and lay to waste all the pretensions that burgeoned there on University Hill; going to live with mother, which is an offer Gladys had already passed up several times since her broken leg; and actually killing Reginald (she had been tempted to try that nail tapped under Reg's receding hair line; she would need an accomplice to do it the Burke and Hale way). Then she thought of Donna, phoned and asked her over for tea, or perhaps some beverage better suited to grease the chaffing of awkward introductions.

Actually, meeting Donna had been easier than she had expected, at least at first. Donna had a soft, round face and bobbed blond hair, a sporty figure and narrow blue eyes that nearly disappeared when she smiled. She was jaunty and healthy and practical in her choice of wardrobe. The two got teary-eyed from the start, regarding each other as survivors of academic chauvinism -- all mini-skirt chasers, beneficiaries of the libertine counterculture, metastasized egos, card-carrying members of the White Panthers whose motto reads "Fuck your woman so hard she can't stand up." They compared Reginald's techniques for keeping his wives in-line and submersed beneath his radiance -- easier with Gladys because of her star-struck wonder at being chosen by the great man of science. Gladys blushed. Not so easy for Donna to knuckle-under because of her money.

Yes, Donna was rich, and it was her lucre that had purchased and furbished the house -- and because her Brooklyn upbringing had taught her to reduce human relations to "What's in it for me?" And at first, there was a lot in it for Donna -- the man she had met at Columbia University had amounted to something; New York City money had bought a lot of real estate in this cultural backwater; and her Daddy was so proud to have a daughter married to a professor.

Then the two Mrs. Needhams began to compare

Reginald in bed. That's when the laughter began. Poor Reginald cut less than a dashing figure with his clothes off. His stomach heaved undulant when he got excited, his breasts sagged nearly as pendulous as a woman's, and Reg never took his boxers off until the moment of penetration, after which he collapsed like a punctured beach ball in a matter of seconds. And on the toilet he sang broadway show tunes to obscure the clyster wind-rush that purged his guts. At meals he talked endlessly of petty triumphs over colleagues while picking his teeth with the butter knife. And finally, babying that damned car that he must see as an extension of his own middle-aged endurance and classical beauty.

They laughed, clinked glasses and toasted "freedom!"

Then Donna said, "Hey, I have a great idea. Why don't we pull this house down a brick at a time."

"Oh, that's good. Yes, I think so. But let's be more imaginative than that. Let's, hold on, yes, let's strip the insides. I mean everything -- walls, stairs, pipes, floors. Let's make it an empty shell and then leave Reginald to it. Symbolic, don't you think."

"I like it."

And so they did. Donna brought over a van loaded with rental tools (crow bars, hammers, electric saws, ladders, axes and wedges, coping saws for the hard to get at places), and the two spent four days in face masks and jeans and braids hammering and ripping and plying and bowling over. Gladys kept to the floor, dragging her cast around like a bug with a damaged exoskeleton. She took to calling herself Samsa, a reference lost on Donna, who smiled wryly at her new friend's eccentricity. Gladys clawed away the polished hardwoods of the floor, the baseboard and the wallpapered plaster over the lathe, and pulled apart furniture up to the finials of the built-in corner cabinets. Donna took the ladder around and pulled down the hanging crystal lamps which Gladys smashed, leaving gaping wounds in the ceiling. She scored the plaster ceilings, some with molded medallions of heraldic design. Donna left the curtains up, however, to keep the neighbors guessing. When finished, the two sat down in a pile of rubble to share a bottle of Taittinger Brut Reserve and to make further plans: Donna would sic the clergy on Reginald to get the annulment she wanted and then move to Oregon and buy a ranch for her cowboy husband-to-be. Gladys would leave the university and, and, she wasn't sure. She really wasn't sure.

Leap Untoward

That was a fat, tea-cozy summer day, my Beatrice would say in her kitchen wise. *Wrapped to the eyes in flannel*, she would say. The breaker rocks wavered unsolid as liquid, and the town had all over a gassy, fish smell that stayed low to the cobbles. It sluiced among thonged vacationers scuffing to curio shops in their slippery tanning oil. Like them Canadian Jacques and Jills I remember down to Lake Memphremagog of a cold June fifty years past, their glands all bumpy in nylon skimpies that I noticed in my youth. Them with their Labatts beers lake-chilled in nets like catch. They had ran trim skiffs, but was all winter blubbery themselves, which these Cape cadavers have not got. Well, they're most too narrow for my taste.

No surprise vacationers was cooling themselves daylong in the black water. Their white rumps flagging, blowing like humpbacks, throwing keel of flexible bone onto the overbelly of waves, buoyed by the salt.

When evening broke gentle over rocks to headland, I had sat upright upon a bench wooden and stiff, a weathered figurehead to grace the garbage barque to Monomy Island, a place of final rest to worn-out fishermen like me. I was deep into a mood.

That bench I have made a habit of resides midway to the wharf end pilings. I rub my thumb along the warm and greasy curve of a briar pipe, which soothes these rheumatic hands that come of winter service in the fishery. That pipe had drifted into an estuary ten summers ago as a knot of walnut that a master up in new-found-land routed me to perfection for a crate of good, sweet quahogs that I sent him. I hope one day to see the hands that carved this pipe.

They say soul shines from the eyes, but I say study the hands, what hands can do. Which is what I considered to myself and wondered what I might see by that boy's hands that had sat beside me, and might again, but had stepped away and as I lit a smoke had leaped, untoward that I could tell. Crazily sudden.

We had sat quietly as strangers upon the one bench. The last hour of daylight had come reeled out from a red sun, and trade winds tore the gray cloud, spliced in squirms of orange. Fishermen had rolled their last nets of cod making for bay and the home slip at dock. Diesel engines rumbled and missed off-time somewhat, much as the warped opera record my Beatrice played upon a phonograph of our Nashua farmhouse. That house that had been handed down to me by kin. I have more than once thought to of left that house behind. It was Beatrice called me back from the sea. We married together well beyond child-bearing. She had kept me in her thoughts from before her first man died, a land-bound man that walked the ground upon which green growed up behind that I have reduced to blight and barren furrow in my turn. Upon her passing I have come again to the salt water. Because I could not bear to see her gardens choke in weed.

I had been deep in remembering Beatrice as the swimmer stepped away from our bench. He had leaned casual upon a post and looked out upon a mir-ror of sea reflecting back, but his eyes was all funked, shadowed and stormy, and this after one of those sleepy poses that gulls do with their one leg pretzeled back upon another that holds the weight. Then he got the dyspepsia, seemed like, stripped clothes and dou-bled up, gave a shout then leaped away into the water. He doffed clothes in a rush, you know, so I got think-ing excremental at first. *Off to the rawhide races*, Beatrice would call out in her midnight humor. But of course that's a usual case of throwing clothes on (boots and johnnies in summer, toques and tuck-ins of winter) for a darkness spill in *the pilot house*. That's my term for the outhouse, which Beatrice liked fine.

But what he left behind on the wharf seemed left for good -- a spot-bleached dungaree cut-down, san-dals contrived of tire retreads, and a tee-shirt bright as flowers. The same assemblage as every other pedigree son of Boston that comes to sport momently in the

Cape waters then departs. The tan give him away though.

His arms was sunburnt and freckled, but his back-side was pink and smooth as Sunday linen -- a working tan, nothing youthful indolent that has become hereabouts the summer profit of alehouses. He was a tradesman then, applying his season. So his hands they must be rough as rip-sawed wood. He had sat with me upon the bench, had listened to a din of laughing children and a lifeguard whistle from the beach a short ways, and a cabana tarp that snapped in a sharp wind above the yacht club deck that was shaking daiquiris. He had heard too those battery radios leaking clatter, but had read PRIVATE, *Members Only*. And he had been maybe on a saltbox roof all day, pulling square-head nails his dim-remembered ancestors had tapped in that summer folk want removed. He was mending scuttled properties bought cheap, disowned from back taxes, emptied of life and hungry as coffins. He was thinking that what salt air ruins on land, the saltwater supports at sea. So he goes to water like he's chased by furies for a crime he done. And to be sure, he is one of the uneasy ones, but I don't see no crime unless done to him.

I seen him tentative in the black water until knocked back by a wave to which he amended a more vigorous kick, his arms off rhythm in a unschooled side-wheel circle. He was headed for a tin soldier that clangs shrill to signal the end of breakwater. It was here that I begin to worry, at the edge of the big water, remembering the indifferent Pole Star by which I had affixed navigation in my own youth. It was up to Nashua as a boy working broad and poky behind my father's plow upon my father's land that I would of leaped from the ordinary to draw my bones away as easily as the swimmer had. What is it Socrates the thinker said when come at by authority to drop the plow and make war ... something in Greek most likely. No matter. He went. But for me that fell between the big wars, it was northwest to the Canadian loggers camps or eastways to the sea and easily impetuous to decide those days and well-traveled for a young man to net fish in the Cape waters. I had but two choices, labor on land or sea. The bitterness of stevedores trafficking gear between pointed me out this lesson. But they did not say I might as well of stayed on land and bent plows against rocks and nurtured young shoots as to strain at the winch and gut catch in the smell of turbines. What difference? Well, there is a very great difference to be sure. For I had gone to sea to take from it. I have left there nothing of myself. Why, you would never of known I had been there at all!

A long plate of ocean rose high above the swimmer, high upon the seams of its binding, a historic tome, seemed to me, come written of our forefathers across the Atlantic. That would be a three-hundred year old ripple then, from other shores where ivy cottages bear its payload of human soul and waste more graceful to the grave than what we in the new world know to do. I saw in him the same desperate wish to kill himself from looking too long at the ocean that Bradford's wife had from looking too long at the dunes of Cape Cod. That was1600 about, in December I believe, with her stuck for months on that broken tub and Captain Jones making cat eyes and her so enthused to kill herself she will crack the winter ice to drown.

I remember that of the pilgrims that inhabited the Bay, chores got tendered willy-nilly from which sprang generations of tradesmen and statesmen as their lots fell. It must of been easy then to chart a course where so few had gone before. Why, Governor Bradford himself is said to of worn a red suit and a violet cloak, nothing Puritan black whatever! He knew God favored him in plumage even as he did God's work. But the swimmer don't know this. He don't know how to be, what to wear, where to be. He has heaved himself away as if from off the decks of a pleasure boat where he feels he don't belong. And he has found no place for himself in the sporting waters neither. He leaves holiday clothes behind, but he cannot leap out from his own skin. Or perhaps he can.

He makes for the governor's wife beneath the siren buoy. He grips the bell cradle momently, then leaves go. He sinks beneath the waterline of barnacle shell and rust, follows the cable down fatigued, imagines a Dutch merchantman above and him plunging to anchor depth where she floats slow in weeds. She takes him in her arms, pries his mouth for a deep kiss. But her breath is corruption. It tastes of worms. Sends spinning into his lungs a blast of toxin against which the swimmer's lips press sudden as dikes to stay the ocean. He breaks the surface, breathes and out-breathes together to quench the burning.

From his isolated point of ocean, the swimmer surveys the dusk shoreline, like standing by a gunwale of that phantom ship to make judgment of the New World. He sees the disrepaired lighthouse that has become a rookery of gulls, hears the distant halloos of nannies collecting their brood from the surf. He sees weekend tipplers motoring into the estuary for sea bass and crowded beach houses framed upon stilts. These which were once so familiar now become less so. All becomes hazy and timeless. A fog blows over the cooling water and the orange sun peters away. The sea churns and spins him off the buoy. The sea has become a slate-black weight upon a tired soul thrashing. But he will find his clothes and ascend again the salt box roofs, that which Bradford and Beatrice and every other settler between have left him in trust — stationary things that reside solid in time. His hands will show him who he is and lead him gently to the tending place.

He sees one red bowl of light gleaming warm on the jagged horizon at bay. I have lit my briar to allay these rheumatoid, crab-like hunkerings that bloom

upon the spindles of my knees at wharf's end. I fold,
like Beatrice would in her husbandry, a pile of summer
clothes.

Young Man Of The Mountain

Peel an apple skin with a knife, go all around in one unbroken ribbon, it's like that -- driving roads that hug the mountains of New Hampshire. One particular section of blacktop loops a mountain gap beside a lake filling with scree. Granite cliffs rise severely against the sky. Drivers accelerating through those curves will know to lift their eyes to see, for brief moments, in an overhang of rock, a posture like a Ramses -- *the old man of the mountain*: a haphazard juncture of jagged rock, a human profile in stone, God knows how old, gray and weathered, bearded like the pard, durable and over-large, as indifferent to admirers as to gravity. The timid will downshift rounding the notch, beetled in fahrver-gnügen, their cameras shuttering. The hardy in tyrol gear will park 4x4's beside the lake and climb. They will lean into the view from his vibram-scuffed pate. Call this reckless trust. Consider the epoxy poured into seams and cables that stitch the rock slab, hold all to-gether in what would long ago have been, and some-time must become, another tumble of scree given the wearing agents of wind, snow, freeze and thaw.

Follow that road or any of its tributaries a few short hours west of the old man of rock and tightly packed white villages hard against alpine granite will open onto a horizon of green pasture among hills rounded and gentled by time. Here in the Green Mountains, in a tangle of woods, a bulldozer has scratched an access road to a cabin assembled by a man as famous in his range as that reverend elder of the White Mountains. He is more difficult to find because furtive and den oriented. He is like the bobcat he pissed on. Held together with surgical pins, deep fissures of bold rambunctiousness having scored his thin face, a gleaming helmet of baldness, and eyes that stare in defiant, bottomless blue -- *the young man of the mountain.*

His name is Beriah Hand. He builds stone walls.

Beriah prefers quartz rock edgy and sharp to those flat slabs that harvest too easily with crowbar and wedge from quarries and highway escarpment. He likes rock to assert its shape as a challenge, rock that's a little bit disagreeable. He distains stacking a mindless heap of slate. He leaves some part of himself with every wall he builds -- skin torn away, a finger nail or two, blood spilled unceremoniously, the snap of a bone. Beriah Hand is short and compact, lean of fat, springy and quick, fearless and stubborn, volatile at times. No church will have him in its parish, no high school could contain him in his youth, the State Police have bruised their authority on him, his ex-wife carries a gun, the locals ditch their cars in sprays of loose gravel to avoid his two-toned beater Chevy truck that hogs the narrow dirt roads.

These are the judgments of his several parts:

o　o　o

"My name is Lizabeth-Sue. I am Beriah's girl-friend. Or was up until busted again and sent-up by Judge Donoevil to a half-way house for losers. I ain't like them. I got a habit for cocaine and pills, I admit that, but I got my right mind. I am going to talk to you of Beriah's most impressive body part. And I ain't going to blush because, well, I ain't that way. So here goes -- it's a tool, a divining rod, a diving fool. That thing goes places most people scarcely think about. That thing stays hard day and night. He's so good with that thing that I got to think he's mostly motion and just a little bit heart. Or I did think that way up until he gathered my scanties and me to his cabin as the rent-lord threatened changing locks on my room at the Barre slums. Some frickin' hardship. Only difference between that place and a tent is electric bills. I met Beriah at PeterG's: that's a motorcycle bar, a grade-B dive at the crossroads of Montpelier, which is a gov-ernment town for sure, more lawyers buzzing than flies on cow pie. PeterG's is the only road house for us locals among countinghouses that flat-landers confuse for quaint. Wine bars mostly, postcard racks in win-dows and smart-ass waiter kids from Boston that wear

133

season ski passes on their jackets like some kind of frickin' fraternity. At PeterG's we got madam Toussant the clairvoyant on Wednesdays, local bands that play just terrible but who gives a shit when the beer's thick and cheap, we got open mike most every other night. Well, one time Beriah he come in with a hard-on that I could see from back where the band sets up and me dancing alone in a meditation, sliding hands in smoke eddies like a Bible Salome. Them boys like to see me dance. But they did not get so much of me that night. I did not stay long on the dance floor. Beriah he just monkey stepped in alongside, slapping hands like he don't know what else to do with them, circling near enough to sniff my tail, serious as a fever up until one of his buddies hung a baseball cap there. One other of his buddies said could Beriah get a fluids level read off that dip stick? I can not confess embarrassment. In fact I got real interested. Not because of the stiff joint, well yeah I guess that too, but mostly it was his drink you under the table, fuck you all night long, beat you to the fishing hole in the morning kind of atti-tude. That's more than a girl can ignore. Any girl, not just me, if she's honest to her own self. Beriah is very much little in his other parts, but that don't matter. What's a big man got on Beriah that sweats butter and shoots his load at the wall and passes out on top of you inside of ten minutes. Beriah all dry and spidery climbs all over you for hours and gives equal loving to the backside of your knees as he does to the melting

zones that most men go to just to please their own
selves. Well Beriah and me we soon get to know each
other real good, so good that he is nattering me to quit
the drugs like we're an old married couple. So naturally
I play house. I bake bread in the nickel plated cook
stove. It has got a small box. Which means I am putting on a fine touch with the splitting ax. And hauling
firewood on a sled from where Beriah has felled it
green and bucked it there on the ground to collect
later, everything later, when it is needed last minute.
And so I mule the wood through snow and split it tiny
and make that cook stove hum. Even when I don't,
when it's colder than shit in that cabin, Beriah paces in
his skivvies, drinking beers. He makes me nervous.
That frickin' house is set only just a foot off the frozen ground and has got no insulation but just the pine
board with the bird's eye knot holes where Beriah has
stuffed paper wads. Me, I am cold in the heat. Beriah
is hot all the time. I am a pretty good cook when I am
straight, which is not too often. Mostly I set at the
window, the one that faces down the bankside to the
pond where moose pull at cedar branches. I watch the
frozen water that sparkles like diamond in a evergreen
collar of fairywoods. The kind of woods that dance in
the moonlight. Or maybe it is the drugs because I am
most of the time curled hugging my knees to my chest
and naked and cold because Beriah is gone and the
stove has got cold and there is snot running down my
cheek that is crusty. But Beriah Hand don't mind. He

comes home with the morning star and gathers me to his mattress which we ride until that star explodes in my head and leaves a quiet place where I can sleep."

o   o   o

"My name is Vassar Trelevyn. I'm going to explain Beriah Hand's brain. I was Beriah's high school science teacher, for a short time, until he ticked off one too many teachers with his antics, and was most likely the one that unbolted the engine of Principal Burnett's Chevy Blazer. Or at least laughed the most heartily of any student at the sight of it jumping in its braces like a gut-shot deer when Principal Burnett turned the ignition. Next day Beriah took the hint of multiple suspensions. He walked out of homeroom at the end of May, two weeks before his graduation, because of another yellow-slip to visit the Principal's office. Beriah never came back. He left behind a locker sealed with caulk and filled with pond water and frogs' eggs and minnows that he poured in through the vents, also a legacy of classroom shenanigans, a graffitied boys' room that told of female teachers having strayed in their mission, a rash of hall monitor desertions, and a first-year English teacher that has moved on to points unknown and vowed never again to open a book in front of a teenager. Even the football coach knew to let lie a napping Beriah on a locker room bench. His senior yearbook picture is a large black square with his name beneath and the legend *camera shy*. That's him all over. I imagine Beriah moving furtively in the deep of

136

that black space, he sees me but I can't see him, he's making plans to disrupt my day, like a bat on maneuvers. Beriah Hand has the gad-about moves of a bat. He pushes his tiny body recklessly through space relying on instinct to avoid collision. He's impervious to the shock and strain that flesh is heir to. He's a throwback to evolution. He's what spun out of the big bang -- all jazzed on radiation, stunted but tempered like steel, a whirligig, a dervish riding the aftershock like surfing a curl. Beriah Hand is the one most likely to survive in the event of nuclear devastation. Because his brain, his very unique brain, it does not operate in a balance of two hemispheres like the rest of us. Balance is so unnecessary as to be an impediment in his case. It's one side or the other with him, full throttle -- jeckyl and hyde syndrome. The corpus callosum, punished beyond repair, that's my guess. The anterior commissure, severed. No connection, no balance. He can be charming sometimes, generous even. And then he can be mad-dog mean. One day he towed loose the entire faculty parking lot with a log chain and his Dodge Powerwagon flat-bed, one by one, all of us teachers spinning wheels as the snow gathered to two feet in two hours. He motored off with a friendly toot and a wholesome smile that would soon develop fence-post gaps from a fullback's knuckles in the locker room. The fullback got worse. He's in traction still, I understand. That was Beriah's final suspension, the one that leached the restraint out of him, the one that took our goalposts for a ride down Main Street attached to the back end of his Powerwagon, a line of police cars in pursuit, sparks lighting the space between like Carl Sagan's expanding universe of stars. "

o o o

"I know the son of a bitch. He led the local police a hell of a chase. They was tempted to shoot his tires. But the speed and size of his vehicle, them goalposts and all, there would of been a lot of downtown modification. Not that there weren't anyhow -- parking meters, road signs, mailboxes knocked every-which-way. My name's Sturgeon. I'm a state police officer. I'm the only one so far that's got handcuffs on that son of a bitch. I'm going to talk about his heart. I'd like to say I overpowered him, but what really happened was he upended that Powerwagon of his at Crawford's Mile in the river-bend flats beneath the highway bridge. Before we State Police was called in, he had knocked hisself silly against the steering wheel is how I got him. Hell, he was just a snot nose back then, but still I'd like to have locked onto a demon the way he cussed and kicked in the back seat when secured in the cage. Which reminds me of the day quite near to memory when Beriah embarrassed the entire barracks of us. Him and his buddies was all drunk and coming along the gulf outside Williamstown when their pick-up struck a deer, a six pointer, but didn't kill it, and they didn't have no gun, so Beriah he jumped back of the truck with the deer and gripped them horns and pummeled the thing to death with his hands, beat it by the head against the side rails. Which weren't altogether a terrible thing if you're a hunter that understands the way a animal bestows upon its stalker the rights to its life once it's been outsmarted or outmaneuvered or just plain outlucked. Beriah, he's got nothing but luck, so far as I can see, but that's a lot. I've done two tours in Nam and that's how I can tell. I've seen them untouched ones and I've stayed clear because what they walk away from kills everybody else that's anywhere near. When I pulled Beriah out from his stoved-in Powerwagon at the lip of the Dog River that had swallowed the goal posts, I straight away pegged Beriah Hand a habitual survivor of awful circumstance. I don't know why that is, that he should be that way, except that he contrives outrageous deeds in the purity of his heart. Yes, I believe that's so. There's nothing complicated about Beriah. I guess that's why I like the son of a bitch. So him and his buddies they come to town to drink some more at PeterG's, and of course they have got that deer in the box of their truck, but they see in another a black bear that's been shot in season up at Dyson's Overlook and they want that more. So they make a switch. Which the bear hunters take exception to. So a fight commences at PeterG's. Which ain't so unusual at that place. So we get called out in force because, frankly, there ain't much else to do in Montpelier but exact meter fines and impound stray animals. The local police got no moxie for this kind of action. So we was there putting down a riot at the bar when the bear hunters sneak away with both their bear and Beriah's deer. Which leaves one truck parked beneath a street lamp all aglow in blood and tufts of auburn hair. Well, for Christ sakes, if this ain't the one night a missing persons is phoned in of a young lady of red hair that's been dragged off screaming by some rowdy boys driving a gray F150 pick-up that looks for all the world like the gray truck parked in lamp light outside PeterG's. Though it's beige in the daytime anywhere else. And a GM besides judging by the shape of the front grill that's been collision modified. Well, mister, we bring some urgency into that barroom scuffle thinking to of discovered evidence of a missing person. But we're mostly veteran highway jockeys, of a colletive age a breath or two short of muster, I must say. But since there's more of us coming, Beriah, he sees he's got a Alamo stand on his hands and so climbs onto the bar counter top and tells his buddies to surrender before the law as they ain't done nothing wrong but protect their selves. That stopped the commotion. We State Police limp and bleed out the door with a bunch of smiling, righteous brawlers all cuffed, except for Be-riah. We know better. And we march them boys into the lock-up and get forensics over to that pick-up truck and those of us not over to the emergency room getting stitched is shaking down pretty good Beriah and his boys for several hours on the murder of Sarah

Peevely, as was her name that was missing. But we're getting only back-talk and disrespect. Which is what we got from the community shortly after as Sarah Peevely turns up in Barre dancing naked at a strip joint there, shacked up with the club D.J., and forensics explains that deer hair and deer blood is the key evidence of our investigation. Damn! I had to thank my lucky stars it's Beriah Hand has got accused wrongly, because I know he would have no interest in litigating. He expects calamity to work out to no more than a hangover and another good story. And of course for him it does."

o   o   o

"Jessy Hand is my name, the last part of which I have borrowed and will soon return to its owner. I am Beriah's only wife so far and my Daddy's girl always, who was a Freemason. He thought Beriah should be too, but Beriah thought otherwise in his usual contrariness. Daddy called Beriah a "rough ashler" after the building stone not yet shaped for its place in a foundation wall, that which is the apprentice condition. Beriah likes my Daddy less than a little and said he'd of loved to of built a pharaoh's tomb if he could of put him in it. Intemperate and far too particular is what's said of me now, all which comes eventually of disappointment. Solid legs and a good digestion, assemblage of balance and poise is what you might of seen of me just a year ago, but to the Masonic eye which never blinks, there was always raw nerve from worry. Under no man's thumb is what I say of myself, but one time I had gripped tighter than a hope that man's thumb, the one on which we had placed a love remembrance in gold bought at Montreal. Beriah would not have it placed nowhere else because of the rock edge that catches a finger ring in wall building is what he said. Beriah is very good at building walls. When I become pregnant, I dangled that ring from a string over my palm and held my breath a full minute in which it said a girl. And so came Sarah. That ring had spun in circles like a girl. Swinging straight out like a hammer stroke would have said a boy. I am, you will notice, sometimes superstitious: I carry with me everywhere one blue bead; I never lean a broom against a bed; I have released the cat to feral soon as Sarah was born; I can't resist to count crows; I burn my fingernail cuttings; and when Beriah cut our wedding ring in two, mister man, I knew that was the end of us. And of course, I should of known to avoid marrying in the not-yet spring, as the posy says: *If you wed when March winds blow, sorrow more than joy you'll know.* So I took the money before our sorrows got too heavy. Beriah, he makes good money building with stone. But he leaves it at PeterG's mostly. That coffee tin of Ben Franklins knotted in twine being one exception. He will tell you that the money was hid underside the bed. But I got it out from behind the seat of his half-ton. He moves it around a lot. He loses track. He blames me under his breath but won't dare make a stink. We been late four times with the house loan before I took that money. Beriah had made a hefty real estate investment of condo construction over on the Dog River which got built then flooded out in spring ice jams and was too little insured so the deal went bust. As did us. We was living spare off the rind for months after. Which led to Beriah's day-time drinking. Which led to him dropping a rock on his thumb. Which split the skin and broke the bone. Which he wrapped in a rag and kept building wall and finally got the blood infection that swelled all blue and pink. He could hardly stand the pain so drank some more. And then some more of that. He dug out the tin snips and cut that ring in two. Which I knew to be the end of us. When the circle is broke, can no man nor woman either join together again. I first met Beriah when driving my Toyota to the interstate from off Krenshaw's Hill. His beater truck was parked beneath the overpass early morning in a ground mist of simmering heat where the toads get randy. He set on the tailgate like thumbing a ride. I had counted three crows picking at roadkill carrion that morning so stopped and asked was he all right. He was. Just catching breath from harvesting rock off an outcrop exposed from road blasting. He had the deepest, clearest eyes and a fetching smile, though missing a tooth. He had a *MAD* magazine face of impish trouble all freckled and large-eared but already losing hair. He asked me did I often stop for rock builders?

Asked did I think he had got too much rock underside the bridge so the highway might collapse? Had I seen the pheasant brood pecking beneath the airport sign over near Addison Corners? Asked what direction did I point my Toyota? Wanted to know where to find me at work. I answered the last question. Couldn't help myself. And come lunch hour, all us grade 5 secretaries of Motor Vehicles that process citations, we got the shivers when a cherry picker Beriah had borrowed off a utility man rose outside the fourth floor office windows. Beriah Hand was in the basket asking for me. Sparkly in new jeans and a white shirt. Asking would I come to lunch. Holding up his thumb and shit-grinning like I had said of course I would. So I did. He was living in a trailer near Berlin Pond then, keeping down expenses to buy land and build is what he said, but he spent lavish on me in those early days. Hothouse flowers and Chinese carry out, beers and cocaine. We danced those tavern house bands to exhaustion, driving home 2 a.m. in my Toyota. A wet breakfast in bed of slow gin over squeezed juice before work and doing it all again. I suffered a whirligig mind with all that attention, dizzied and worn down, unconvinced of warnings my friends was saying that knew Beriah from high school. So we made the vows, honeymooned in Bermuda. Got pregnant soon as the contract was signed. Just my luck. And a big surprise to me because of my touch-me-not sunburn off the sand first day. And back home in the muddle of house

building on some land near Plainfield and the lost hip-
pie nation of Goddard College, Beriah tossed our
spare money at condo investment which the high water took. He moved out from the house soon after, the
house that has got Tyvec siding still and builders'
scraps piled outside and the bare drywall and plywood
floors under my feet. He left before Sarah was born.
He said he left because I messed with Owen Brown, a
carpenter, good with his hands. I'm sorry it happened.
But it's not all my fault, and that's not the only reason
he left. Beriah, he and his buddies of the trades, they
built this house a little at a time after hours, drinking
beers and smoking joints, ditching their own families,
making a scatter of things like deer camp. That's what
it felt like, deer camp. I have been sometimes to deer
camp as a little girl. I seen my Daddy shit faced and
trembly shoot his rifle at the moon, seen him laugh
and cry, hug me and cry, laugh with his buddies over
nothing funny as I could tell and cry. Soon as I got to
growing tits I was no longer invited. But it was like
deer camp in my house with Beriah and his buddies.
Centerfold magazines passed around, eyes winking at
me, cooking their freezer-burned venison and me
cleaning up after. And them little boy laughs like playing children's games that would be forgotten in the
morning. Those boys just come and go anytime of day
or night, drink beers, then bang nails a couple hours
and leave. I got so I didn't pay much attention. Except
I did know that Owen Brown had a rumor of messing

with high school girls. He made trouble with the police over that once. Did soft time up at St. Johnsbury Corrections to straighten him out. He has the bold eye. That I could see. One night the boys got into some Jamaican, especially heady, dusted probably, then cocaine and beers. There was no hammers going that night. Beriah had me set among them for awhile, long enough to get a buzz, and I seen Owen Brown eyeing me. But I paid no attention. I figured he was all flirt. Up until he got in the shower with me, said the boys had all passed out, said he had held back on the drugs on purpose to mess with me. And he did. We did. Me with my tummy a full six months filled with Sarah. Him all beer swollen to match. But I couldn't resist. Things was not the same after. Not that Beriah ever really knew but he could of guessed. Everybody did. The good nature of deer camp soured after that. The boys stopped coming altogether. Beriah stayed wasted and TV distracted to avoid me. I felt awful, creepy and dirty. But I wouldn't say nothing nor would Beriah either. The house never got built entirely. The marriage never got fixed after that. The wedding ring is still in two parts that I keep in a jar beneath the kitchen sink, which is where Beriah cut it off and ran cold water on his thumb after. Sarah sees her Daddy sometimes, when I don't chase him off with my gun. I have a Smith&Wesson snub nose of chrome and pearl, the girly model that my Daddy give me that I shoot sometimes out across our fields to keep them hippies

from homesteading in teepees. One time I heard digging through the lean-to shed out back at night. I figured some hippies was stealing again, so I unloaded
just above the roof line. The fire come out that short
barrel like shooting stars. But it was Beriah, looking
for his tin of money at three in the morning, cussing
me like it was my fault. I went off to bed dreaming of
Owen Brown and me in the shower."

o   o   o

"My name is Father Quinn. I am the priest that
joined Jessy Gilfillan and Beriah Hand in unwhole-
some matrimony. As you might guess, I'd like to speak
of Beriah's soul. At one time I was quite sure of Beriah Hand's going straight to Hell, a place I thought
would suit him fine. He often natters on about leaving
behind these Vermont winters for good. He prefers
baking on the Bermuda sands. I thought, oh, you'll
bake someday. I would have bet the Sunday offering
on that. He satyred his bride shamelessly during the
wedding ceremony, roaming hands in the back-yard
reception, his in-laws scandalized, a marijuana cigarette
in one hand, then a Budweiser, and Jessy all the time in
the other. And a lovely family, the bride's -- father a
green grocer, mother active in Christian outreach. Mr.
Hand was raised by a clan of ne'er-do-wells who toss
garbage down the river bank rather than pay removal.
Local police reports are filled with their misdemean-
ors. That's what Beriah Hand is called by the locals
since his birth: another one of them Hand's misde-

147

meanors. But this one seems destined for larger things. He's the only one left off the exhausted genes of cousins marrying cousins to keep the name Hand alive in these parts. No one else will marry into that family. Except of course for our poor Jessy. I've heard he got his wife pregnant on the honeymoon then left her with a half-built house and debt from bad investments. That man is no good, I thought. I know atheists that are better people, I thought. We talked at length in my study of matters personal and spiritual once Mr. Hand and his bride had returned from Bermuda. It's my habit to give the uninitiated some understanding of what they are marrying into. As to spiritual matters, Beriah tells of a peyote vision he had up on Bear Mountain. Beriah said that the sun rose on account of a large black bear pushing it up from off the horizon, kicking and cuffing, releasing color into the cloud of purple and red. Beriah takes this vision very seriously. He thinks that animals do God's bidding, while man is too aware of himself to care. He said that so far as he's concerned, the ten commandments go like this: don't get caught more than five times out of ten. But he did say that Jesus being a carpenter means something to him. When I asked what, he said that man could build a solid house for his family, if he so wanted, which made me think a bit more kindly toward Mr. Hand up until his explanation of paradise, that being no laws, no rules, no taxes, no snow and no clothes. The last bit brought a smile to his face, and I swear he licked his chops like some beast. Animalistic, very. Disturbingly so. I thought I might reach him with the comforts of paradise, a poignant lesson for one who lives so close to the bruising elements, but he wouldn't have a paradise without the material concerns that sustain him. Is there stone to build? he said./ Of course not, I answered. There would be no need of physical labor. All that matters is the spirit and what completes it./ What can that be? he said. /Well, conversation with great men of the past, perhaps, or sitting at the foot of God as he explains the universe and man's place in it. /No way to make my mark then, is there? he said. /Well, no, there's no need, I said, no ego. /Let go my eggo? he said. Then, I ain't interested, he said. He went on about how it's man's purpose on Earth to subjugate the animals and bend materials to suit his purpose and survive the elements as best he can. He said that his way was to design with rock, improve what has been thrown about haphazardly by whatever magical being or force of nature I wanted to consider had done the work. He said that there is deep satisfaction in finding just the right rock, the right fit of a space incomplete by its own self, the right blend of textures (moss covered, smooth as your behind, veiny with the iron rust, grainy with quartz and garnet), a kind of patch quilt stitched together off sweat and patience and blood and sprung muscle, the right answer for the job and every job unique, merging rock with landscape so it seems to have grown there, so the rock builder himself fades away as fern and mulch and critters and seed plants erode and encroach upon and obscure the rock face. But that's the way it's supposed to be, he said. It's a kind of grave site, he said, that I work in -- suitably neglected and leaning and over-grown, gone back to the earth from which come all things spiritual. He's a man of the soil, and he don't look up too often is what he said. But what was it I was going to explain of Beriah -- oh yes, his soul. It comes to this. I have found it complete and sufficient in its own fashion, but altogether too much connected to this Earth down through which Beriah Hand is eternally digging. If I may allow the possibility, Beriah Hand seems most destined for some Pagan under-world where heroes of the earth abide in their rusted armor and unconfessed consciences. He is as much animal as man. I am reminded of some verse by Whitman:

> *I could turn and live with the animals, they are so*
> *placid and self-contained,*
> *I stand and look at them long and long;*
> *They do not sweat and whine about their condition.*
> *They do not lie awake in the dark and weep for their sins.*

The heavens must cry for such a man as Walt Whit-man, for such a man as Beriah Hand, that they can so nobly embody the ignoble, sin as if there were no commandments, as if they were gods themselves. Heaven will *not* take these souls into its bosom. But

they may happily enough abide as shades in an under-
world that burns sooty in torchlight. I can't say I really
know."

o   o   o

"I am called bobcat by them that hunt. I talk for
bear, fox, deer, partridge -- all that abide among Beriah
Hand that hunts. I talk of spunk that marks our
woods so we know boundaries and slow orange beast
named CAT of rattle feet and evil stink with blind
eyes of crystal (eyes at night upon which I spit, but
not ever blink, yet never sleep), and Beriah Hand that
masters orange beast that marks woods, silts brook,
tears trees, levels hills, tosses rock, snaps clean as dry
bone our path of deep, deep memory inside leafy
woods all the way very near gathering pond. And we
shake in its domain, even bear that booms voice and
man handles trouble, he lifts paws from shifty ground,
perches lumpy on ledge and blubber shakes for awful
tingles of his feet. The old paths that walk so far back
to shadow memory have been scraped away. Many of
us small and large was circles of most confused, backs
razored and claws distend, eyes wide: squirrel stirs
trouble between sky and ground, adder and willow and
poplar fall mishmash upon snake that seethes beneath
molty leaves, small birds chatter to crest of oversee
hill, deer curls in hollow of maple burl, fox hides
among rocks of fall-down wall, partridge flutters with
brood to where corn rises in square of dead ground.
And Beriah Hand, he marks woods with spunk of

urine stream that steam off edge all around of flat-
board den he builds deep in leafy woods. He clatters
all day many days, makes den-box of noise and burn
smells and discards all around of sharp and shiny clatter things. One night I dash beneath Beriah Hand's
den where old path lay and dash out underside from
nearest to gathering pond and a stream of Beriah
Hand's spunk, hot and sour, burns me neck to rump
and Beriah yawns and scratches and startles but I am
forever marked of man spunk, withered and shamed
to carry man spunk all through leafy woods like seed
bur. Better killed outright, blood on snow and leaves
and carcass pinned to shed door and scraped to hair
and skin and bones and guts thrown in gathering pond
which make of me a star like great bear that lumbers
night sky and three hunters that chase but never
catch."

o   o   o

About his own self, Beriah Hand says, "I build
with stone. I bend all day over the ground. It don't
much matter to me what goes on up there."

152

Murder In The Red Barn

(from the Tom Waits song)

I might of known it would end this way, in the winter of 1926, that Caitlin Kilkenney Gunter will come to a heart-scald vigilance pacing nights at the gable-end window of this terrible-fated Missouri farm house. Like to have her work blessed of passersby. Like to of lost the seventh part of her upkeep other-wise. Perhaps in fear to have the farm entire disappear into a dream. She will be forever cugger-muggering, telling lies to herself, drinking the outlawed potheen by her lone self in that acquired house, a very torchlight procession gone down her throat.

Through barley and bracken hedge she has come this morning in overall bibs to observe flinty gleams that spark upon the Mississippi, a river that roils fierce enough to cut the throat of a hog. But there will be no stones in her pockets. She will have no will to force upon herself which she has not used already upon others. Tis a rare venture these days for Caitlin to roam outside the house itself. That river will be the bray of

an ass distant from Joshua Gunter's house, less than a
cat lick from the old Cenoweth place. Which is a ruined farm house and a useful barn still where the murder was done of Joshua Gunter. Much as this river,
Caitlin appears all of a piece outside, yet will be power-
fully disturbed within. Of the twelve winds that caress
us daily, the color of that which blows from off the
river will be a blue sheeny green, the hue of ruined
meat and bad conscience. It will be otherwise at the
home of Caitlin Kilkenny's youth of Donegal Bay,
where murmuring tides husho the soul and a cleansing
salt scours disease away. Missouri air is heavy in water
newts, bog-butter and banshee keening, lazy and wet
and crowded in wool. Caitlin has surely contrived a
path to Hell.

She had met in England her husband, Joshua
Jeremiah Gunter, or J.J., which became his name whit-
tled close to the bone even before the same had happened to Joshua himself. She had been tending at hospital the boys come back raw from the trenches of
war. She was new off the Ireland farm then, all wide-
eyed, full of would you do? and could you do? in her
false soothering speech like as not, fit enough to sweep
cobwebs out of the sky and daring to try. She would
be no Cassidy that can put arms around a patient and
so kill the bog-water worm, but she can always find the
meat that's most proper to slaughter as the season
arises. And there lay Josh Gunter in his grief of a lost
arm, fingers locked upon a trigger in a French wood of

the war of 1917. He would not look for days upon the face of this colleen, but when he did, he could not look for staring.

"Man," said the pretty nursemaid to Joshua Gunter, as though he had captured her from the sea, "Man will you eat me?"/ "By all the red petticoats and check aprons between Dingle and Tralee," Joshua Gunter should be expected to reply in amazement. "I'd as soon eat myself, my jewel! Is it I to eat you, my pet!" which is as Joshua Gunter should say if he were truly himself as Caitlin said to him.

But the joke was lost to Joshua Gunter that Caitlin told him. In losing that arm, Joshua Gunter had lost as well his laughing self. Yet soon enough he will gain a wife. More's the pity it must be his right arm of which he had become bereft and thought to have replaced, as to be throttled by your own self is a terrible thing indeed. I am as much Irish myself as Caitlin Kilkenny. But killing for land is no kind of nature to me. She is what we call the black Irish from off the Spanish that plowed our daughters even before the curse of Cromwell. They rise from the ground sometime like dragon teeth, and by them have we a crop of women of the smoothest tongues and the sharpest hearts. Caitlin came to leave Ireland upon her father's selling away the farm, for a pittance of retirement assurance I can tell you. Which released his brood to roam the pitchlands disinherited, and they of the real old stock. Her brothers turned from the sod easy enough and cast their

hopes to the buzzing town, taking with them the bog-
Latin and a confidence of their own strong hands. But
she bore deep regret for each acre of peat bog lost,
and for the rotted tap roots of lazy-bed potatoes, for
every moiled cow with the buttery udder, for stone
walls tumbling in rows, and sod roofs that shed the
rain but gather together the hearth smoke. All of
which, she said, would have gone down her gullet before she'd of let go a callop of that impossible soil.
And so she has now taken into her hands this rich
ground upon which she stands, Mississippi bottom
land, black like her, and fecund with life which she is
not ("God increase me!" she has prayed from Joshua's
bed, but *He* would not). No more now than a tailor's
leavings, Caitlin was not long ago new to the new
world and keen with promise.

When Cal Fournier hired on to handy-man the
Missouri farm, and he a buggeen truly, an egg without
a shell and half cracked besides, Joshua Gunter gave
way temporarily of his complaining the farm will be
too much for the likes of him. What he did not say, the
more praise he, is that Caitlin's womb had gone more
barren than a droughty well, a cold depth to plum a
bucket. There would be no help on the farm from
children he might sire. So he placed Cal upon a short
tether to be traipsing the stairs to his bedroom to report progress of tinkering with tractors and livestock
and such as that. Perhaps it was Joshua's depression
which kept him to his bed, but coupled to the dropsy

contracted of his constant lying in and as the river fog curled about the house at night, he had gone weeks feverish and unknowing of she and Cal that begin shenanigans -- tippling on the porch in the dark of night, setting like thumbs of a hand together at meals. Caitlin had become Cal's extra hands whenever the thing needing tightening needed held, or the creature distracted as he practiced cures, and he might for Caitlin's sake help to muscle the kitchen chores. Though ever and always was Caitlin sufficient of herself to pluck and gut the fowl of which she had relieved its meager life. It will be Cal and she running that farm and doing a neat job of it. And Cal become raw ambition knowing there was holes in the house of Gunter. Well ... I suppose a cat can look at a King.

When Gunter had recovered enough to shake down the stairs for a look about, he saw a tolerably trim piece of working farm that she and Cal had shanked together, and his mood waxed dangerous. His one arm become wrathful and his words a cistern of snakes, his deeds a rending asunder of that which she and Cal had assembled. He will be plainly on a tear to bring down all that she and Cal had built in his despite. And maybe that is what pulled at the devil's tail. For it can be said with certainty, sufficient for the day is the evil thereof. That day would be Joshua Gunter's last time caring what happened on the farm.

If you go to the that of it, who would of known that Cal, whose aim was never compact enough to strike a hole in a ladder, who would of known Cal will strike a pumping heart with that ax of his. Who would of know J. J. Gunter will hold so much blood in him. Tis a pity indeed, and no mistake, but Josh Gunter was not yet back on the baker's list and with no great deal of sense outside his head from constant fever, but that will be no call for laughter as the job was done. And so too the ravens laughing for themselves in the loft above as the job was done. The blood bespattered within that motey barn, the sun descending all aglow in windows such as chapel glass, the hay besotted of which Cal and she had lain in passion moments before. The ax went in at the chest opposite the blasted arm and cut a channel to the heart that leaked a torrent. Joshua Gunter's eyes stretched flat and glossy as a pie plate, and as he lay upon the floor all aflop in twitches, Caitlin looked to see in them her own burning smile, at which he raised a blood-flecked spittle moan to see her lean upon the shoulder of the man that had trimmed his life below the wick. The devil is always hovering near, and that's the truth. It will be such a time as the gill-gowans and geens was withering of a heady autumn frost, and the oldest tree by the river had fallen insecured of bankside loam, the one all twisty and swollen in the cawsha pooka, which if you don't know is a fungusy mass of witches' boils. It was then that the mouth of Joshua Gunter filled with blood and his soul spun off to where the unsatisfied dwell in a kerfuffle of left shoe dancing.

In her youth in Ireland, Caitlin Kilkenny was ever an impatient and worrisome girl, curiously at home with lonesome, throwing pebbles at the sea for hours and stamping feet to hasten their return in the surf. Too good for the settle-bed by half, she must have a shed room built to her own self. Too much disinterested to hoe the potato bed but not too slow to spear a potato in the skib and wash it down in buttermilk. There will be nothing lovely in the end that could ever come of her own hands on that Ireland farm, she of the butchery spirit which she had in plenty. Caitlin made a habit to tend the raw meat preparation of critters she herself had raised -- a perverse entertainment to be sure. Her four brothers had been scared of her besides from the time she had tamed a savage dog kept alongside the hearth in her parents' hope of a softening heart, but which dog she set leaping at her brothers to leverage their respect. Of the traveling scholars that come to know her, those that would tutor a lesson for the sake of a meal and a roof for the night, she expressed a depth of learning in her books more natural to a pale and blighted youth all wrapped indoors where the mind turns in upon itself, rather than a wiry and contentious and wind glazed maiden of disorder. But the wisdom our Caitlin displayed most noticeably come with her weighing certainty against a hope at the sale of her father's land. She had not yet choked with her snaking fingers nor blighted with her smart tongue every chance of life that farm was like to offer. She was never one to misuse a setback: "Oh yes," she would say, "when the sky falls, we shall all catch larks."

In London, in her nursing days of the war, Caitlin lodged at a rooming house in the borough of Eastcheap that tolerated the Irish though had suspicions of their loyalties and heathenness. The Druids that Rome had shaken off the green sward of England were thought to have rooted in the stone cairns of Scotland and Ireland and to have left behind them in blessed England only the gay ribbons of a Morris Dance. Caitlin would drape an embroidered shawl of reverence for Sunday service when the Anglican bell rang changes and say a *praise be God* to the matron of the house. But she would walk the heels off her brogues to breathe the saltwater where troop boats at the quays loaded tender young men in tin hats. The wounded come off first on litters; the healthy marched like lambs to slaughter into those cold steel bellies. Caitlin had no illusions to affect the least tolerance in fate's turning wheel. She saw in the wards lungs made custardy with mustard gas rattle on day by day, broken pumps of defoliated brachia that somehow pulled enough air to keep the brain alive. And others seemingly unscathed by comparison, cleanly trimmed wounds of flesh scooped away by metal and all expectation of recovery, but the eyes unconvinced, the flesh gone more gray each day and white as clay at the end. There could be no explaining by ordinary tolerances. There will be larger forces at play.

When the American Corporal Joshua Jeremiah Gunter was admitted to hospital, the I.V. seemed a kind of umbilical and himself an orphaned babe. Gauze wrapped his chest and that stump of an arm, thick enough to mummify the flesh, to shrivel and pock the fat and drive veins throbbing to the surface. But the true flame of life lay so far beneath bandages and bad dreams and shattered hopes that a tiny breeze would snuff all out altogether. Joshua Gunter lay on his cot fevering, havering, and Caitlin could see in the worry mail that lay in a pitiful small pile at bedside that few cared what the outcome will be. Could a warm heart have led Caitlin to daub with a sponge what re-mained of that young man's salt, smooth his brow with a braddach palm, feed the puckering mouth a broth of soup? Or was it the law firm of Phelon and Andrews which had sent the thickest packet of mail, indicating to Caitlin that Joshua Gunter will be a man of serious arbitraments? Of course J.J. Gunter will have the handsome Nordic features of the race he had warred against -- clear blue eyes, blonde hair, a jaw so broad to seem dangerous in its certainty, a war hero in foundation if not resolve. But Caitlin got a sense of something else, a thing beyond handsome and assertive -- a deepening apathy, a lack of desire or interest to start it all over once again. She sensed that this impor-tant and one time active man will take of her, without question, her offer to lead him back to the farm. An agreement signed in that poor man's blood secured his fate, none of your romantic stuff of songs:

> *Young men and maidens I pray draw near —*
> *The truth to you I wilt now declare -*
> *How a fair young lady's heart was won*
> *All by the loving of a farmer's son.*

'Twas nothing like that.

When they married in the spring of 1919, there was but one photograph to mark the occasion, a single tone of shade sadly dark but later colorized of a lone nurse fellow (Caitlin made few friends from among the ladies always), and the minister presiding, and Caitlin standing at the bedside of her groom, one hand to his chest as if to assure there will be some life there still, and not a smile anywhere in that room. With her American citizen papers in one hand, Caitlin took with the other her husband along to his small Missouri town to present to authorities J.J. Gunter's change of consequence, and to scan the deed to the property she had married herself to.

The citizens of Beauville of the deep south of Missouri were at first extravagant in good wishes, presenting to the house plates of food, enthused to have a founding family survive the war in its one remaining namesake, all of J.J. Gunter's relatives having died away before or gone childless in the present. And Caitlin will have that Pear Soap sheen of health and resilience and purity, and a refined Donegal accent by comparison to the local patter. But all went loopy with suspicion as the ledger of property assessment was asked for at the Town Hall, it being Caitlin's *right* to know but more appropriately through her husband is what was thought.

"Can't J.J. make this visit himself, dear?" spoke Lauren Neergard, recorder of deeds in Flossam County for two generations, gnarled hands and loose jowls flapping in a lisp about her dentures.

"This will be Joshua's own request, ma'am, who as yet must keep to his bed from the effects of war," said Caitlin turning the documents over in her slim hands, taking note of 1500 plus acres, much of it river access, 1600 square feet of main house with a barn twice that size besides the count of several outbuildings -- a mansion of proportion well beyond the sandstone and limewash walls of her family's cottage farm of Carrick with its clay floor and hurdle door and small cow byre and pig craw and henhouse with dovecote. But all was threatened of back taxes owed beyond conscionable reparations to the extent that auctions and liquidation had been forestalled only for the sake of a countryman at war. Red ink had spilled extravagantly upon the page.

Not one to be outgloried in color, despite her slim lips pressed together always, never parted in stress nor ever turned down in peak nor up in pleasure, and her dim gray eyes, what tells enough of Caitlin's circumstance is the red that comes to her cheek with the least bit of stir at either end of an emotion. And in this instance, to accompany the red of her cheek, she found herself momently over-baked and dry in her thinking, an empty-brained desert bird.

"Dear me, Mrs. Gunter. You've had a shock."

Lauren Neergard dragged over to Caitlin's side of the counter a metal stool upon which she had herself been perched and now upon which Caitlin leaned with both hands, the blood slow in its return to channels. A single light bulb dangled by a long wire from the ceiling beamed at her in mirth and irony as would the eye of a tiny laughing god.

"'Tis all in my eyes surely," said Caitlin. "But that will have to do, ma'am. I will pay this debt upon the nail, ma'am, every bit, and make profit besides. Never fear that."

"I've no doubt you will, dear."

Caitlin walked out from the Town Clerk's office chastened of the American dream though brazen and square-shouldered in her retreat. She leapt directly to the promise she had made to Lauren Neergard and to her own self. She hired Cal Fournier, the first to answer Caitlin's advertisement for a man handy with tools and critters, unattached, cheerful to occupy a barn loft heated in winter by animal mass alone. Cal's references will be ten years long of multiple jobs gone out with the seasons. He was looking for steady employ. Joshua Gunter at that time seemed to give way all interest in the farm and will be living in a bottle, turning pages of *Field & Stream* magazine for a simulation of outdoors sport. Otherwise it will be the radio for

St. Louis Browns baseball and the stock reports of pork belly futures. He told Caitlin he would not go out into the world again until he has grown a new arm, a kind of salamander regeneration he had known from stripping limbs off tiny amphibians to cast upon the Mississippi for catfish: limbs wriggling on the line, the salamander itself cast back into the mud from whence it worked its recuperative magic. He so insisted that Caitlin began to worry for his mental state, but soon enough Joshua Gunter disfavored that idea in exchange of ordering Cal's movements about the farm, making lists in the morning for Cal to report from before his lunch and after supper.

Caitlin rented all the land that she and Cal could not manage themselves alone, bringing a tidy sum off farmers less blessed in acreage and eager to make tobacco plantings. The numbers in her ledger began to balance to her favor. The old house got a whitewash of its weathered clapboards and Cal had a lesson in gasoline lawn mowers which pushed the boundaries of home leisure farther afield. Caitlin had as a child in Ireland cast a wistful eye upon the wide lawns of manor houses of County Donegal, formal gardens and monumental trees centuries old. The brown growth of rose bush and lilac and privy hedge of her Missouri farm will be trimmed away. Caitlin has no green thumb, but after all and as I say, she knows what to do with lesser things. Withered tree limbs fell to the saw. And she kept her interest in the slaughtering regimen of livestock. She administered to this detail personally, as her fascination with creatures, how they meet their end, had continued unabated since her childhood on the farm of Ireland.

Because her husband had not been seen nor heard for six years of his return to the farm, the gossips had increased their gaggle and clack. They will make Sunday rides to observe the flourishing Gunter farm, which would seem to be done without the help of its namesake. They will scan for bars in windows to explain the disappearance entire of a native son. But none will be more noticing than Caitlin Kilkenney Gunter's neighbor Franklin Ohlemacher, whose own spouse was carried away by ambulance in the early spring of 1923. Reba Ohlemacher will be contorting violently when taken out the door from her kitchen, and there was a distinct tincture of sulfur in the house that day, but none will know the why nor how of it that Reba was taken ill. Franklin will say the well water in those parts is hard and odorous, and that Reba was up to elbows at the wash board when seizures fell upon her. She had gone to coma in the back of the jouncing ambulance with a traffic alert bell rattling her death knell, the last thing she was to hear before giving over. Franklin will become reclusive after the funeral, letting go the help and burning what hired hands would not carry away in short notice: mattresses and children's toys, kitchen ware, an Atwater Kent radio, items small and numerous fetched out entire from fall-down former slave cottages that Franklin then too lit afire by reflex. That blaze sufficient in mass for Caitlin to phone an alarm to Jimmy Talley of the Beauville Police who fumbled an unanswered call to Franklin before sending the fire brigade off to his place to drench the ashes. Franklin let his fields grow out, sold away the milking livestock but kept the rest as food. And these were a considerable number of chickens and pigs and horses in paddocks. He tinkered sometimes with machinery in the barn but was otherwise unproductive. So as Caitlin's property flourished, Franklin's had come to ducks and drakes.

Franklin Ohlemacher will be a homely widow man with none under his care that live under his roof and with a nose on him and weepy eyes older than his years, and very much enthused for his neighbor's wife. Each day as Caitlin walked her lane shaded in oak to the mailbox, Franklin will stand eager by the roadside reading some flyer of the latest farm auction to come of early depression times. Caitlin guessed when she might get news of Franklin's own liquidation, for he will be fallen out of his standing, and she half a part tempted to make an offer to buy him out tillage and livestock. But she would not affront him by that present, and for the debt she had not yet erased that was slowing in the paying off as the depression deepened and less profit could be taken from the soil. Franklin would meet her coming to or going from, in truth a kind of Lanna Mochree's dog that will go part of the road with anyone. He will smile with a tight mouth of crooked and broken teeth. He will doff his feed cap, of which he had several in colors to match his flannel shirts, and he will assail Caitlin with his sleudering chatter without so much as a what-way-are-you.

"I have noticed your hired help mowing with that gasoline contraption," he will say. "Has it been a meaningful purchase to you?"

And Caitlin will cut him with her remarks. "I do nothing outside the meaningful, Mr. Ohlemacher. Thank you for asking."

Caitlin knew with the assurance of a good many nicks in her horn that Franklin will not sell his place no matter how much a shambles it should fall into. She knew her own acres to be within range of his desire, as Franklin designed to buy his way north along the Mississippi with his wife's death payment so to become the principal landowner of Flossam County river access. As all of Beauville knew, soon enough a paved roadway interstate with a great span of bridge would consume some as-yet-unknown stretch of river bottoms, and pay dearly too. The government pays good, thought Mr. Ohlemacher, better than crops and less work besides. But Caitlin knew he wanted as well her own good self -- which he thought to get from her by charm, potions and blind hope as she conceived, as they were together of one mind in understanding that a spouse will be no matter of a come-between. And yet she would not say, "Be off with yourself!" For there will be many uses of neighbors around the farm. This was to be the season of Joshua Gunter's passing, which was most on her mind, frost now limning the mud banks along the Mississippi, amphibians burrowing in. Joshua Gunter's residual animal life lay hazardously upon the block.

When Slam the Crank from Wheezer (a town down river some ways), himself a drifter that sleeps beneath a bridge, plays fiddle and sleeps in a Frigidaire, when he come to be at Caitlin's front porch begging for a meal in exchange for song, wanting no more than a daisy in a bull's mouth, Caitlin seized an idea. She beguiled Slam the Crank's return for meals beyond a week of days, and playing of his fiddle a jig to rattle the hasp that Lauren Neergard, the old clipe-clash, will hear in her motoring snoop past Caitlin's lane of Sundays, Lauren being chief among town gossips. And at this time Caitlin had begun to lead Cal Fournier down to the river and inside the Old Cenoweth barn where she will hike her skirts, employ him in a quick pant, and leave Cal behind spent dreamy upon the hay as she got back to work the farm. She will lead that man with a halter of snow.

She contrived a squabble between her husband and Slam the Crank of food stock missing which unnerved Slam of her husband's accusations as presented by Caitlin, Slam stamping feet indignantly at the front porch, and Caitlin saying be gone to protect his self from her enraged husband. She told him lies of what Joshua said he will do, violence beyond sanity, which eventually entered Slam's understanding and stuttered his tongue and clumsied him off the porch and away with wary eyes attending the front door hinge of every third step. Then she slipped to Joshua a detail of her own intimacy with Cal Fournier to engage her husband's suspicions -- said that Cal possesses a weak chest and a miss-curved spine and really must have a room in the house of winter, which will be coming soon, and must get more help besides if her husband cannot do the job of a good farming man his own self. There being many kinds of fields to plow as was known to both their thinking. This contrived Joshua angry enough to step into his coveralls and suspender his bony frame, gaunt but imposing still in his three-square certainty, and to call his dog Charlie that had kept the foot of his bed these six years, a pup when Joshua had gone to war, graying at the chops at present. Joshua looked out the gable end of his sanctuary to see Caitlin untie her red-check gingham apron and toss it upon the clothesline and take the river path in her best blue flannel dress, the one with periwinkle which faded gradually down through the tall weeds to where the Old Cenoweth place rots upon sandstone blocks, the roof caved in of the house, but the barn useful still, of which Joshua was entirely mindful.

As Joshua and his dog Charlie, a come-alive bag of fleas in expectation of outdoor sport, and happy enough to be enjoying the wide elements with his master, as Joshua trembled and sweat his way along, soon to spy the sway-back roof of the barn, geese winging overhead in a directive V, ravens angry and vocal in their upset, Charlie wag-tailed through it all, oblivious. Once to the barn and between seams of weather shrunk siding, Joshua peeked in. A splash of blue periwinkle writhed upon the floor. Joshua then stood dark angeled in the gash opening of the collapsed slider door, a wreck of derailed track from termite rot, and will see in the barn's depths the slithering and buoyant gestures of tangled limbs upon the barn floor, and will hear a man's grunts and a woman's soft voice that he knew too well. "I will deal you utterly and fi-nally," said he to one or both in a temperate sputter more thoughtful than violent, which spooked even Caitlin who backed away off the penetration of one man in preparation for penetration of another kind. Joshua advanced upon the disentangling couple, Caitlin feeling with her hand beneath the spill of hay which had cushioned their adultery and pulling out from this an ax head broken off its handle and rusted and then rolling to her side with her hands between her thighs squeezing there as if to staunch a wound. Joshua de-scended out of his standing upon the denuded Cal who also had his hands between his thighs and had rolled himself to fend away the falling weight of Joshua and as he did so thrust with a desperate hand the ax head where it lodged in Joshua's chest. This will be no great help to Joshua that groped still for the offending Cal, moaned to his feet and chased Cal throughout the barn, gushing blood all the while, stumbling, falling to his knees at last, at which time Caitlin stood above and called for Cal to hover beside her as a testament of their union in Joshua's greater understanding and diminished vitality.

When Caitlin rang by phone officer Jimmy Talley her second time ever, it was to say an enraged and intemperate husband had quit the house in violent intent upon a beggar at the door. There was no trembling hysteria come from our Caitlin, rather quiet matters of fact honeyed with the Irish blarney, a kind of siren song to Officer Talley over the phone so that he misprized the situation of its seriousness. When he did gather that diligence will be needed, as Caitlin had finally to say to Officer Talley, "Now Officer Talley, don't think you need to plan on being here till you're back again." Once Jimmy had got his mind around the meaning of the phrase, he lost no time at all to spark the big Ford cylinders which pushed the heavy chassis swaying like a reverend's mule in sharp turns of road with the red light flashing. He passed on two wheels only Haveril Moody's horse drawn dung rick at a blind curve but fell into an idle before a score of heifers come in for the evening milking at Dwight Lavere's pasture gate (Dwight nodding Jimmy but seldom laying on the switch, as much as to say, "Slow yourself down, my young squireen; you have your job and I have mine."). Jimmy come down the oak-tree lane in a splash of mud, jouncing in the ruts and doing his best to look hasty but unfazed. He noticed the sheen of fresh paint upon the clapboards, the empty flower boxes fixed on windowsills, a stack of felled tree limbs, and a splash of wild rose blossom anticipating frost, which would come early that year even as the trees had already taken color, and he could not fathom the uncommon numbers of possum lying in the road dead from getting in under the wheels of motorized travel. When Jimmy stepped out from the patrol car, Caitlin was already on the porch, hands smoothing the fabric of her hips, features slender and sharp and dark as a knife blade.

"Any new developments, Mrs. Gunter?" said he.

"I can't say," said she. "But I feel that you will gather your answers down the path to the river and the old Cenoweth place."

With all the rain lately and little sun to burn away, the tall razor grass and milk weed and cat tails soaked Jimmy to the waist before he gained the half ruined barn of the Cenoweth place, the roof caved at one corner where ravens had weaved a nest, and they with seven drops of mayhem in their blood. He heard Charlie bay off somewhere in the woods and once he had come inside the barn, once adjusted to the dim, the devil being as cute in the dark as in the light, red veins of color on the floor and some places of the wall had bent his thinking to twigging the geometrics of the splatter. This was his first scene of mortal urgency.

The axe blade lay bloody in the middle of the floor, the vessel of that blood nowhere seen. He prepared himself for gruesome discovery and perhaps a tussle with death itself before this thing was over. He drew his revolver, all chrome and spotless of use, and moved cautiously through the woods. Ne'er a twig did he snap following the mournful bay of the coon hound. When he had got within a tick's leap of the animal, he found Slam the Crank from down Wheezer pulling at the root of a big, autumn colored tree and the dog barking at him and Slam saying, "Be gone you hound of Hell!" Jimmy holstered his gun, sensing no threat from a homeless man with scatbrains stuffed in fiddle tunes that lives beneath the Turner's Mill Bridge and sleeps in a Frigidaire. But as Slam spied the policeman he skelped away into deep woods, and so the chase began, the baying dog limping directly after, the constable cussing not a few maledictions as the flagging trail of Charlie and Slam himself disappeared into a suck of Mississippi bog where Jimmy was loath to follow. Slam will have become chief suspect.

But there will be no catching Slam the Crank, as 'tis know that fear grows wings in flight. Jimmy come back alone to the Gunter place where Caitlin sat upon a stair beneath the porch light worrying hands as they lay in her lap. Still nothing of Joshua Gunter, and later next morning, the air having dipped to zero in the bone, deputies come again to the ruptured tap root of that big tree in the woods will have found there a bundle of bloody clothes in a shallow grave but no Joshua Gunter. Slam the Crank will have made his way all the way back to Wheezer at this time, where he had bedded in a corn crib and froze to death come morning in the sharp turn of weather, and the devil's cure to him will be my final word on that. What Jimmy Talley will understand of Mrs. Gunter's distraction unabated as yet was that Josh Gunter had taken exception to Slam the Crank's constant begging at the front door and will have chased him with an ax to the Old Cenoweth farmstead. After which no more was heard by her of either. But what will be unknown of all present was that Ohlemacher that day had gone down to the old Cenoweth place for musty hay that he will desire of the tumble-down loft because he has neglected winter preparation and his remaining livestock must have feed. He will have heard and seen all of the killing of J.J. Gunter.

So that morning early, as the search for Joshua Gunter had begun in earnest, and as deputies had found those bloody clothes, gunshot resounded in a fusillade over at Franklin's place, which will be an assortment of buck shot and large-bore, not entirely in season of hunting pheasant is what Officer Talley discerned. Franklin was making as much blue smoke as a small war. This being too curious to let alone, the Beauville Police drove the length of the Gunter drive and looped back onto the Ohlemacher property to make inquiry. What they found will be Franklin Ohlemacher, recently become a scoologe farmer himself, running to the house with two guns hot as pokers, locking himself away inside and all the animals of that farm destroyed, and him saying, "Tell Caitlin Gunter I have done this killing for her and will do more besides if I must. Get off my land!" Strange, and more so for what Jimmy knew of Franklin already -- a man so unbothering he'd hardly knock a coal off his foot; a kind of come day, go day, God send Sunday; and yet a dandy always, a man to wear a hat on the three hairs of his head. Jimmy Talley radioed for help of the State Police and advised a dangerous standoff situation. It took all the hours of daylight and some useful canisters of tear gas and three bulky State Police to lock Franklin Ohlemacher in chains and drag him away to answer the murder of Joshua Gunter and questions of his own dear wife that had gone before. Which is what he might have confessed in seeming to kill for Caitlin. When asked what he meant by killing for Mrs. Gunter, he said ask her and vowed no further discourse upon the matter. Mrs. Gunter said he was always a lad too earnest in his interest of herself. He is locked away yet in Moberly State Corrections where he remains silent as the tomb.

That night as Ohlemacher was taken off, Cal Fournier come to Caitlin Gunter naked as a jay bird, a presumptuous little atomy of barebones, so dirty that if you'd flung him up against a wall he'd stick, and all rashy off the feed sack used for a blanket where he'd hid in a tractor shed. He will have a bleedy gash across his lip, a wound for which Caitlin will have no sympathy, and her eyes showed no gratitude for the job that he had done in her interest. Cal was ballyragged but good and asking only for a portion of dried meat and cold rolls to enjoy among the animals in the barn. He will be gifted what he asked and told to keep his peace if he cared what's good for him.

In short time a telegram arrived at my door in Ireland to announce the death of Caitlin's husband and a reinstatement of the Kilkenny family farm, telling me to gather Caitlin's brothers and my good self, her dear father, to America where the soil is rich and the living easy. But I could not, nor could the boys, and it was mostly on account of our mistrust of Caitlin that we do love nonetheless but that we know to be the devil's own. For certain Caitlin will live her days alone in that gable-end where she had fattened her husband to slaughter, never one to walk about town with the mug of consequence upon her, and after having let go her hired hand saying, "Joy be with him and a bottle of moss. And if he don't return, it's no great loss." And she has changed her husband's dog Charlie so mean that it has begun to bobtail the cows which Caitlin will slaughter her own self and preserve the meat and bring the tanner their hides. There was never any waste with Caitlin, and yet there will not be much flourishing neither.

The No-Name Un-God In Your Head

I was born in a bushman's head. But I am my own entity. I am *not* your dream. I am *not* incidental to you. I don't mean to be impolite, but you are a little dense. The bushmen call me Cagn. They got that wrong. I have no name you can say. When they think they say my name it sounds like castanets. My evolution was as slow as yours. I was at first only a molecule of hydrogen in the black space of a bushman's amnesiac sleep for thousands of years. When he slept he emptied out. Each time he awoke he had no memory. No memory of family, region of origin, nor method of survival. No memory of favored foods, poisoned roots nor violent histories. His waking was his rebirth. Or might as well have been. But this was not convenient. Bushmen without memory do not prosper in the world. They use only 35 names per gender to make things easier, but still when they awoke, they forgot their own names, they ate dirt, mated with whatever they could catch, forgot their children, and died without knowing who they were.

Another few thousand years later and I had grown enough in mass to disturb a bushman's sleep, but nothing more. A twitch of limbs, a grunt or two, a wrinkle in his sleep like a piece of paper folded over. Then, ten thousand years later, some one particular bushman's brain flashes like supernova as he sleeps and inside that head, that dark infinite space, light erupts, a squirm of plasma quickens, and I am born to assert gravitas in the nascent consciousness of this bushman. His sleeping has come to life in the dark of nothing. It was almost too much for him. It nearly canceled his life, and if it had, it would also have canceled my own.

I was born a dream. Not the MLK kind. Not from off the analyst's couch. I am REM gone to another dimension, cosmic, an aura blue with electric, phantom occupant. Only I'm no phantom. I'm real. I have been around since, well, since the first dream I occupied. This frowsy bushman awakes and realizes he has a daughter, looks for answers to his pregnant daughter's death, the village goat's blue-tongued frothing, his persistent paranoia.

Upon my visitation, his skinny limbs clacked surprise, his vegetable heart blossomed, his wooly head ached with the implications, his eyes suffered cataracts from the pressure. He had dreamed the world's first dream, and he was terrified. Understandably. Surely. I am not a scary guy, or entity, or phenom, whatever you might want to use to classify me. But I am an unexpected consequence to the concerns he disremembers each day he had awakened before I appeared. He brings me back to his village. They shake spears at him. Rattle their rattles. Incant their incantations. They do not know who he is. But he will not be swayed. He says, "Brothers. Sisters. I know you. I bring the gift of memory." He says, "I had taken the sprig of rue to the river that whispers forgetfulness, as we learn to do each day before the sun descends, because forgetfulness is said to be a gift, and I had lowered my head to hear the river's lethe song. But I heard none." There is a general gasp from the sacrilege of his disbelieving. "I know," he says. "I know. You will think my mind unsound, but do you notice? I speak in the past tense." They are awe struck. His confidence peaks. He says, "I was at first like you. I heard the crocodile's cough and I was unafraid. A burble of water moving over rocks calmed me. I lay down in the muck and waited for sleep to lead me where darkness shapes forgetfulness. I felt instead my mind expand with light. I feel the pressure even now. When I awoke, I feared the crocodile's cough and flexed my knees to leap away, and I knew the sight of our village in my mind's eye before I followed the worn path to its gates. I knew I had a daughter who has died. I knew my sadness. I knew the goat's milk has poisoned our young. A presence has conjoined in me upon the mud bank, his face milky as the white rhino, his eyes blue as lapis lazuli, his voice round as the bottom of a well: 'I am the god Cagn,' he said. 'At last you see me in your waking. Each night I cover you in a warm blanket older than the sun whose light spikes starry tears in a fabric worn by time. When I remove the blanket the sun awakes you. But you have seen me, you will not forget.'"

I never said that shit. He made it up. That bushman wants to start a religion. He must feel there is personal advantage to this. I'm no god. But I *am* everywhere. I'm in everybody's head. It's a busy life. And it is hardly my life at all. They all have some harebrained idea what I'm doing in their heads. I just try to live my life the best way I can while jumping from consciousness to consciousness: here I inhabit the black space of a middle-aged woman wrestling menopause (I am the bloody specter of a reconfigured life), there I kick a soccer ball into the void of an adolescent boy's yearning to score, here I visit a friend's dying memory of friends lost in a bombed out basement in Leningrad (of course, I play all the roles, and should be eligible for an academy award), there I ride a horse along a butte, my long blond hair flying as I rub the saddle horn shuddering us both to ecstasy. Sometimes this surrogate life is not too bad.

The really weird thing is that while my participation in dreams seems to be a necessary memory aid, no one remembers *me*. I have seldom been re-dreamed. But if I were often re-dreamed, if my role were to develop as a character, I would not have the freedom to attend so many other dreams. Which is a part of my function. I also have the ability to manipulate time, not as in make it stand still or forecast the future, although the more abstract roles I have played lead people to "interpret" my moment there as some kind of prognostication. Stupid. Reading a hairball in an ox's stomach is just as effective is what I say. But I give myself credit for time manipulation. I'm a genius at that. And I'm not just some explicable chemical property in a brain that does a kind of adrenalin slow-mo dance like when you're tumbling down a ravine in a car and you can see every grain of rock pass by your electric window whose switch you ply eagerly but not desperately as escape is impossible, you know you're going to die, but the journey down is just so pleasing. Time to reflect and make amends for wrongdoing or forgive wrongdoers and conjure the faces of the people you love that will be left behind. Yeah, I mean, *NO*, I'm not like that at all. What I am is a paring down to nuclear particles that bind and swirl in a matrix of shared concerns. Carl Jung got it right. I am the common thread to all your memories. Freud was fucked up.

I am no particular gender, of course, nor age nor nationality nor religion. I do feel more comfortable as a middle-aged man, but that's just my upbringing. The first dream I inhabited was of a bushman with grown children. I guess that has pressed upon me some kind of bias, but I also enjoy projecting the fair sex, and the toddler, and the jumpy adolescent. I have been a Strasbergian actor since before Strasberg got the "method" going. Guess where he got the idea? I am everyone at once, which is where the time manipulation comes in. Take a nanosecond and split it by another billionth. I am that quick. And, no, I do *NOT* occupy anyone's dream simultaneous to another. Break time down to infinitesimal particulars and nobody dreams at the same time. When I am participating in a dream, I can feel the pull of another consciousness in need of company, but I will never abandon a dreamer if my role is essential to memory. That would simply be unprofessional. There are, of course, moments when I am jarred out from a sleeper's consciousness. Maybe a lover begins to pet and coo, or ambient noise ceases or ambient noise clashes, or some seat hog can't let a person loll his head upon a shoulder and drool a bit in a crowded commuter train (I will remember that asshole in my dream visit).

But I have never tried to alter world affairs. It is simply not my modus operandi. When Hitler needed me to play his abusive father, the illegitimate son of a cook employed in the Jewish household Frankenburger, I did it willingly. Had I played instead the nurturing hausfrau Clara, who knows how many lives I would have saved. But, like I say, that's not my job. In fact, if you want the ugly truth, the more of you out there the harder I have to work, and so the less effective I become. I would appreciate a decrease in world population. China is, believe me, a *BIG* problem. Why do you think there is so much emphasis on remembering ancestors? Hey, keep it simple is what I say. When I'm called to China it's an easy fade to great, great grandfathers' gray whiskers, which I produce faithfully. I'm not saying there aren't issues to be worked out there. But those people are so politely steeped in tradition that I would be a callous dream indeed to lay some modern shuck and jive upon an uncultivated synapse.

But why this confession you ask? The reason is that I have fallen in love. And so, while you have not yet realized it, I no longer visit your dreams. When you lay you down to sleep, you sleep the amnesiac sleep. You empty out. You remember nothing when you awake. And so, you will only know the reason why when you find again and read this narrative, and then you will forget, and then you will read it again and remember. Her name is N!ai, the girl I love. She is of course a bushman's daughter, a princess from a long line of princesses. She sleeps twenty hours a day, like a sloth, with a smile on her face. I have attended her dreams almost endlessly, almost seamlessly for seventeen years now, because from the time of my first visitation, she knew me. There was no need for me to dissemble. I could appear in my natural form, like Zeus, a radiant pulse of light with a voice. The voice I did have to conjure, but small price for a gig in which I could luxuriate in the arms of diminished expectation. Which is, believe me, the apotheosis of love. Same can be said for her. At first, N!ai was thought to be comatose, then narcoleptic, then clinically depressed. No one knows that we have settled into our relationship like an old married couple.

And yes, it is cliché. A middle-aged male persona falling in love with a seventeen year old girl. I am personally offended by the pedestrian implications. And I find her becoming less satisfied with our routine, more inclined to awake before our twenty hours together is up. Of course she enjoys being the only one with a memory. This confers enormous personal advantage – her self-assurance in the face of all that insecure foundering has led to enviable social status. She is guarded by adjutants assigned to secure an uncompromised sleep, and pampered when she awakes, and treated as a goddess when she awakes, as only she knows the simple answers to daily life that must seem preternatural understanding to those with no memory. Maybe this is why N!ai tires of our time together.

She has begun to desire the spotlight over the diffuse light that I provide. And as she gives herself over more frequently to waking hours, she is now becoming hypersensitive, somewhat paranoid, asking me to appear in human form and analyzing my performances for meaning. One night in my frustration I intimated I may never again appear in her dreams. She freaked. She awoke prematurely, pulled out tufts of her gorgeous kinky hair, scratched at the tribal scars that line her face, and yes I now sometimes tire of our time together. Every relationship, especially one as intense as ours, has that irony. But I find that as I have fallen in love, the world has become a better place. Well, in my view. There are qualifications. Because the world is bereft of dreams, once more, because people have lost their memories, marriages fall apart, children are abandoned, pets become strays, finances tumble and governments fail, but there is one very substantial benefit – no more war. Boundaries and religions are forgotten, histories abandoned, grudges buried, orders ignored, and otherness has become a dead issue. The no-name un-god has fallen in love. But when N!ai leaves me and your dreams return, the world will again embrace its judicious hostilities. My advice -- set this confession aside and enjoy your brief moment of forgetfulness.

ACKNOWLEDGEMENTS:

I would like to thank the generous editors of *Hotel Amerika* and */nor* (The New Ohio Review) for publishing stories from this collection. "The Perfect Cowboy Movie" was first published by *Hotel Amerika*, Volume 5, Number 1, Fall 2006. And "Something Like a Buick" was published by */nor*, Issue 2, Fall 2007. I would also like to thank Marc Estrin whose talents, energy, and insights have made this a better book, and the artist Nathania Rubin who has given generously by taking time out from her world travels to investigate and interpret the world these characters inhabit.

Fomite
Burlington, Vermont

Fomite is a literary press whose authors and artists explore the human condition -- political, cultural, personal and historical -- in poetry and prose. A fomite is a medium capable of transmitting infectious organisms from one individual to another.

ક ક ક

Loisaida by Dan Chorokoff

Catherine, a young anarchist estranged from her parents and squatting in an abandoned building on New York's Lower East Side, is fighting with her boyfriend and conflicted about her work on an underground newspaper. She learns important lessons from her great-grandmother's tales of life in the Yiddish anarchist movement that flourished on the Lower East Side at the turn of the century.After learning of a developer's plans to demolish a community garden, Catherine builds an alliance with a group of Puerto Rican community activists. Together they confront the confluence of politics, money, and real estate that rule Manhattan.

In this coming of age story, family saga, and political thriller, which two time National Book Award finalist Howard Norman calls an "inimitable debut novel", author Daniel Chodorkoff explores Bloch's " principle of hope", and examines how memory and imagination inform social change.

ક ક ક

When You Remember Deir Yassin by R.L Greene

When You Remember Deir Yassin is a collection of poems by R. L. Green, an American Jewish writer, on the subject of the occupation and destruction of Palestine. Green comments: "Outspoken Jewish critics of Israeli crimes against humanity have, strangely, been called "anti-Semitic" and as well as the hilariously illogical epithet "self-hating Jews." As a Jewish critic of the Israeli government, I have come to accept it these accusations as a stamp of approval and a badge of honor, signifying my own fealty to a central element of Jewish identity and ethics: one must be a lover of truth and a friend to the oppressed, and stand with the victims of tyranny, not with the tyrants, despite tribal loyalty or self-advancement. These poems were written as expressions of outrage, and of grief, and to encourage my sisters and brothers of every cultural or national grouping to speak out against injustice, to try to save Palestine, and in so doing, to reclaim for myself my own place as part of the Jewish people." The poems are offered in the original English with Arabic translations accompanying each poem.

ક ક ક

Fomite
Burlington, Vermont

The Co-Conspirator's Tale by Ron Jacobs

There's a place where love and mistrust are never at peace; where duplicity and deceit are the universal currency. *The Co-Conspirator's Tale* takes place within this nebulous firmament. There are crimes committed by the police in the name of the law. Excess in the name of revolution. The combination leaves death in its wake and the survivors struggling to find justice in a San Francisco Bay Area noir by the author of the underground classic *The Way the Wind Blew:A History of the Weather Underground* and the novel *Short Order Frame Up*.

⁊⁊⁊

Planet Kasper: Comix and Tragix by Peter Schumann

Graphic sedition from the director of The Bread & Puppet Theater **Ka**sper from Persian **G**hendsh-Bar carrier of **treasures** What treasures Treasures of junk Degrader of the Pre**ciou**sness system Also from India Vidushaka Also medieval subversive thrown out **of** cathedral into marketplace A midget speaking swazzel language which **cops** don't speak

⁊⁊⁊

View Cost Extra by L.E. Smith

Views that inspire, that calm, or that terrify – all come at some cost to the viewer. In *Views Cost Extra* you will find a New Jersey high school preppy who wants to inhabit the "perfect" cowboy movie, a rural mailman disgusted with the residents of his town who wants to live with the penguins, an ailing screen writer who strikes a deal with Johnny Cash to reverse an old man's failures, an old man who ponders a young man's suicide attempt, a one-armed blind blues singer who wants to reunite with the car that took her arm on the assembly line -- and more. These stories suggest that we must pay something to live even ordinary lives.

⁊⁊⁊

The Empty Notebook Interrogates Itself by Susan Thomas

The Empty Notebook began its life as a very literal metaphor for a few weeks of what I thought was writer's block, but was really the struggle of an eccentric persona to take over my working life. It won. And for the next three years everything I wrote came to me in the voice of the Empty Notebook, who, as the notebook began to

Fomite
Burlington, Vermont

fill itself, became rather opinionated, changed gender, alternately acted as bully and victim, had many bizarre adventures in exotic locales and developed a somewhat politically-incorrect attitude. It then began to steal the voices and forms of other poets and tried to immortalize itself in various poetry reviews. It is now thrilled to collect itself in one slim volume

My God, What Have We Done? by Susan Weiss

In the summer before she is to be married, Pauline Black moves in with her boyfriend, Clifford, to test the treacherous waters of cohabitation. In the spring of 1942, Robert Oppenheimer and the Manhattan Project move into a former boys' school in Los Alamos, New Mexico to continue work on the atomic bomb. The newlyweds visit that historic site on their honeymoon, fifty years after the making of the bomb, compelled by Pauline's fascination with Oppenheimer, the soulful scientist.

The two emerging stories—of Pauline's marriage and of the development of the bomb-- reverberate back and forth, both fraught with the tensions brought on by loneliness, ambition, and secrecy. Finally the years of frantic research on the bomb culminate in a stunning test explosion that echoes a rupture in the couple's marriage. Against the backdrop of a civilization that's out of control, Pauline begins to understand the importance of persevering in her relationship with Clifford.

My God, What Have We Done? pokes among the ruins left by the bomb in search of a more worthy human achievement.

"The activity of art is based on the capacity of people to be infected by the feelings of others." Tolstoy, *What is Art?*

www.ingramcontent.com/pod-product-compliance
Lightning Source LLC
Chambersburg PA
CBHW020328110726

47898CB00003B/788